How had they been found...*again*?

"We've got to go. Now!"

Ethan's urgent growl sent Lara's pulse skyrocketing.

Lara snatched up the baby and the diaper bag, then opened the bathroom door. Ethan stood outside, grim-faced and gun drawn. He ushered her and her precious cargo up the narrow hallway in the back of the store toward the emergency exit.

"Go!" Ethan whispered.

Ethan's warm hand pressed between Lara's shoulder blades, hurrying her, even as a strange man's voice from the front of the store called out their names.

She hugged Maisy close and charged for tree cover. A masculine shout came from behind her. Not Ethan. Then a gunshot with another loud report close on its heels. Enemy fire followed by Ethan's response?

No time to spare a backward glance. She plunged into the woods, twigs snapping beneath her feet and pine needles raking her body.

Another gun blast, and a pained cry sounded in the distance behind her. Ethan? *God, please no!*

A bitter metallic tang filled Lara's mouth. This was what terror tasted like...

Jill Elizabeth Nelson writes what she likes to read—faith-based tales of adventure seasoned with romance. Parts of the year find her and her husband on the international mission field. Other parts find them at home in rural Minnesota, surrounded by the woods and prairie and four grown children and young grandchildren. More about Jill and her books can be found at jillelizabethnelson.com or Facebook.com/jillelizabethnelson.author.

Books by Jill Elizabeth Nelson

Love Inspired Suspense

Evidence of Murder
Witness to Murder
Calculated Revenge
Legacy of Lies
Betrayal on the Border
Frame-Up
Shake Down
Rocky Mountain Sabotage
Duty to Defend
Lone Survivor
The Baby's Defender
Hunted for Christmas
In Need of Protection

Visit the Author Profile page at Harlequin.com.

IN NEED OF PROTECTION

JILL ELIZABETH NELSON

LOVE INSPIRED SUSPENSE

INSPIRATIONAL ROMANCE

LOVE INSPIRED® SUSPENSE
INSPIRATIONAL ROMANCE

ISBN-13: 978-1-335-72223-2

In Need of Protection

This edition published by arrangement with Harlequin Books S.A.

For questions and comments about the quality of this book, please contact us at CustomerService@Harlequin.com.

Love Inspired
22 Adelaide St. West, 40th Floor
Toronto, Ontario M5H 4E3, Canada
www.Harlequin.com

Printed in U.S.A.

Recycling programs for this product may not exist in your area.

There is no fear in love; but perfect love casteth out fear.
—*1 John* 4:18

To all the protectors who risk their lives
for the innocent and vulnerable.

ONE

Lara Werth gasped and lunged upright in bed, heart in her throat. What was that sound? The hair-raising wail wound up a notch. A baby was crying in her house? Then her shoulders relaxed. That's right. She had company.

Her best friend from high school, Isabelle Storlen, or at least that had been her maiden name, had suddenly showed up last night. The long-lost friend rang Lara's doorbell just after midnight with her three-month-old baby in tow. Izzy had said she was on the run from her abusive husband, the infant girl's father, and had the bruises to prove it. She'd driven twenty hours straight from their home city of Chicago to Lara's house in Jackson, Wyoming.

What else could Lara do but offer mother and daughter asylum until morning when they could call the police? At least calling the police is what Lara had wanted to do right away, but her friend had adamantly refused. Maybe Izzy would be more reasonable this morning? But why wasn't her friend rousing to take care of her baby?

Lara's bedside clock said 6:01 a.m. Right on target with the time Izzy had predicted her daughter would wake them all up. Lara rose and donned her slippers and robe, then padded up the hallway to the guest-bedroom. Knocking, she called Izzy's name. There was no answer except for an increase in the urgency of the baby's wailing. Lara cracked open the door and peered inside. The bed was made—almost like it had never been slept in. She stepped fully into the room. No one was present except little Maisy in her infant seat, bawling and kicking.

Next to the baby carrier sat a large bag Isabelle had brought in with her—a diaper bag, judging by the images of baby toys embroidered all over it. Atop the bag lay a short stack of papers. Lara snatched them up. The top sheet was a handwritten note that said "I'm sorry. Maisy is safer with you. My husband will never suspect she's here. Look after her for me and tell her that Mommy loves her."

The bottom dropped out of Lara's stomach. The message couldn't mean what she thought it meant. Izzy hadn't run off and left her baby behind, had she?

With a dry mouth, Lara turned to the next page. It was an official document with a heading that nearly stopped her heart. "Minor Child Power of Attorney Form." The boilerplate form looked like it had been grabbed off the internet, but it was fully filled out, signed and notarized. Her name, Lara Werth, was neatly printed in the spot for the individual delegated as power of attorney for "custody, well-being and property" of minor child. This couldn't be real. People didn't dump their children off with unsuspecting near strangers, did they? Because, after all these years, she and Izzy *were* all but strangers.

Didn't the parent need the consent of the person getting the POA before executing a document like this? Lara searched but found no line requiring her signature.

Lara turned to the next sheet in the small stack. It was a one-page will—again boilerplate from the internet—that named her, Lara Werth, as guardian of Izzy's child in the event of Izzy's death. A chill gripped Lara. Isabelle must truly be frightened for her life.

Did the father have no parental rights? If not, he must be a more dangerous person than her friend had told her last night. Lara's stomach churned. Perhaps she should have insisted that they call the police.

She flipped to the final page. It was a list with step-by-step instructions about the care and feeding of little Maisy. Lara exhaled slowly. This was good. Yes, she could do lists. Lists were her friend.

Lara laid the papers on the bed and reached for the wailing infant, but the clamor of the doorbell stopped her. Who could that be? Had Izzy rethought her outrageous plan and returned for her daughter? Had to be.

"Hang in there, sweetie," she told the crying infant. "I'll be back in a flash, hopefully with your mother."

A pacifier lay in the car seat, next to the baby. Lara grabbed it and popped it into the child's mouth. The crying subsided. The doorbell rang again, long and loud, as if someone was jamming their thumb on it and not letting up. She could understand Izzy being anxious to be reunited with her child.

"I'm coming!" Lara called out as she hustled to the foyer and opened the door, a greeting for her friend on her lips.

Her smile faded as she stared up into a pair of steely eyes set in a granite face. But it was the gun in the man's hand, pointed straight at her, that sent her heart into gymnastics.

"Give me the kid." The man's thin lips hardly moved as he spoke, and the creep factor escalated to a new level.

A second male figure, tall and muscular, charged onto her lawn from behind the cedar hedge that divided her property from her neighbor's. This one carried an even larger weapon, trained on the man who held the gun in her face.

"Drop it, Seton," the second man said in a flat, no-nonsense tone. "Deputy Marshal Ethan Ridgeway here. You're under arrest."

The first man snarled a swear word, swiveled slightly toward the threat and reached for Lara with his free hand as if he would grab her and use her as a human shield. *Not happening!* A scream tore from Lara's throat even as her fist flew out and connected with the man's shoulder. He staggered, and she ducked away and slammed the door. A gun went off and then a second shot barked on the heels of the first.

A male voice yelped, and something heavy thudded onto the porch. Her assailant getting the worst of it from the deputy? A gun battle was taking place right outside her front door. How could this be happening? Lara's arms and legs turned to useless appendages frozen to her body as her pulse thundered in her ears. From the guest bedroom, Maisy's crying began again, but she couldn't attend to the child yet.

"You're safe," hollered a deep voice from outside. "We're taking custody of the suspect now, ma'am."

We? She'd seen only one deputy running onto her lawn. Maisy's continued crying tugged at her, but Lara needed to call the local police first. She didn't know these people outside her house. Lara darted for her phone in the charger on the table beside the sofa. Her 9-1-1 call took only a few seconds, and after the assurance that help was on the way, she hauled in a deep breath, the first time she'd fully filled her lungs since she opened her door. The creeping dizziness in her brain began to recede.

A firm rap sounded on the door. "Are you all right, ma'am?"

"I'm okay." Her voice quavered. "Who's out there?"

"Deputy Marshal Ethan Ridgeway and my

partner, Terrill Reed. You don't need to worry about the guy who accosted you. He's disarmed and cuffed."

On hesitant feet, Lara returned to the door. "I'm going to open up to the length of the chain, but I expect to see your credentials first thing."

"No problem."

She opened the door and peered out to find a pocket folder inches from her face, displaying the official documentation of a deputy US marshal. Her gaze lifted from the folder and to the man's blue shirt, where a badge gleamed. At last, she looked into the deputy's vivid hazel-brown eyes. He had blond hair and a strong face with well-defined features. Youngish, maybe a few years older than her twenty-nine years. Under the strength and calm of his expression, tension eased from Lara's muscles.

"What is going on?" At least her voice came out firm this time and not a half octave too high.

"Let me in and I'll explain, ma'am. We need to work fast and get you ready to go. It's not safe for you here right now."

"Go?" There went that extra-high tone again, but really, this was too much.

She had a screaming baby on her hands, a gun had been poked in her face by a very scary stranger and now she was about to be carried off by the US Marshals Service, no less? How had her neatly sculpted world suddenly been wrenched off its axis?

Ethan stared down into one-half of the young woman's pale and drawn face peering out at him from the gap allowed by the chain. Her multihued hazel eyes narrowed. Then she shut the door, the chain rattled and the door opened fully.

She wagged a cell phone at him. "I've called the police and requested an ambulance."

"Good," his partner, Terry, said from a crouched position over the wounded gunman, who lay groaning on the porch. "Not sure we need the police, though."

"The locals are more than welcome on the scene," Ethan told the woman. "They need to be apprised of what's happened in their town. Would you tell me your name, ma'am?"

"Sure, if you'll agree to stop calling me *ma'am*. I'm Lara Werth, and again, I'm asking what's going on here."

Ethan assessed the woman in front of him.

Late twenties or thereabouts—several years younger than him. Her shoulder-length corn-silk hair fell in loose waves around a heart-shaped face. Petite in height and frame, she stood not quite as tall as his chin, but her fierce expression would give anyone pause, particularly if they witnessed the mean right jab she'd delivered to the thug who'd held her at gunpoint.

"I'm not sure what part you play in our case, Ms. Werth, but we followed the man who attacked you across the state to your house. We believe you have what he wanted."

"And what might that be?"

Wails from deeper inside the house answered the question.

"Vincent Drayton's granddaughter," he said.

All color washed from Ms. Werth's face. "*The* Vincent Drayton? The international gunrunner from the news?"

"That's the one."

"But Izzy told me Maisy's *father* is after her, not her grandfather."

Ethan took a small step forward, but Ms. Werth gave no ground. "We need to speak to Isabelle Drayton immediately. Please ask her to come out here or bring me to her. We have intelligence that she is in danger. She—all of you—certainly need our protection."

Ms. Werth frowned up at him. "Izzy's gone. She left the baby with me."

Gone? Ethan's heart fell. "When did she leave?"

"Sometime during the night. Come in." Ms. Werth jerked her head toward the interior of the house and stood aside to let him pass.

As she shut the door, the scream of sirens began to draw near outside. Ethan paid them no mind. Terry could handle the local police and EMTs. He followed his hostess into a neat and clean living room furnished for modern comfort with tasteful rustic touches.

"Wait here," she said. "I'm going to tend to Maisy and change out of these pajamas. Then we need to have a talk." She disappeared up a hallway.

Ethan frowned. Why had Isabelle Drayton involved an innocent outsider in an incendiary situation? Then again, maybe she believed leaving her baby with someone else while she led the pursuers away was the best method to protect her child. Things hadn't worked out that way, though. Drayton's people had been right on Isabelle's heels, and she'd brought danger to the doorstep of the home where her baby was now stashed.

The sudden cessation of Maisy's crying brought Ethan's head up. Had something happened? Tension ebbed as Ms. Werth strolled back into the living room. She was dressed in navy capris and a button-down blouse. A set of papers was clamped under one arm as she cradled an infant, who sucked noisily on a bottle.

"This must be Maisy," Ethan said. "We'll have to take her into federal custody now."

"Take her?" Ms. Werth lifted her chin. "Not without my say-so."

"I'm afraid you have no legal jurisdiction—"

"I have documents that say I do. Help yourself." She nodded toward the sheaf under her arm.

Ethan took the pages and studied them. "You've accepted power of attorney for Maisy Drayton?"

"Izzy showed up at midnight last night, and I gave her and Maisy a room to stay. This morning, Izzy was gone, but she left Maisy and these papers. The document says that at this moment, *I* make the decisions regarding Maisy's well-being. I could even become her permanent guardian if something happens to Izzy."

Ethan set the papers on a nearby coffee table. "Then you can legally turn the child over to the marshals service. She'll be well looked after, I promise you."

Ms. Werth blinked and looked away. Signs of indecision?

"You have no attachment to the child nor she to you." Ethan pressed his advantage.

Ms. Werth's gaze flew to his, and her eyes narrowed. "How do you know anything about what attachments have been formed?"

"I guess I don't, but—"

"I need to understand a lot more about the situation before I hand her over to anyone else's care. You can't come in here and swoop a child away willy-nilly." She thrust out her chin. "I'm sure a bunch of federal deputies are going to change her diaper with one hand and hold their guns in the other. A baby needs a caregiver's full attention."

"Whoa!" Ethan lifted his hands, palms out. "It's not like that. A social worker will be assigned to—"

"A social worker is going to care about Maisy more than I would?" Ms. Werth's tone had risen and sharpened.

Ethan's jaw tensed. He must be losing his negotiation skills, because this chat was going sideways fast.

"Please let me explain," he said.

Ms. Werth's glare dared him to try.

"Maisy's grandfather has taken up the hunt for her on behalf of his son, Ronald, who recently escaped from the maximum-security Stateville Correctional Center near Chicago. The US Marshals Service was hoping to pick up Ronnie's trail by locating his estranged wife and daughter, but Isabelle and Maisy were on the run by the time deputy marshals arrived at her apartment. Her place had been trashed, and there were traces of a struggle and some blood."

Ms. Werth nodded. "Isabelle arrived here bruised and limping. She didn't say who attacked her. I just assumed it was her husband since she said she was running from him."

"As the deputy marshals exited the apartment," Ethan continued, "they spotted Seton, a known felon, leaving the area in a hurry. Deputies followed him, thinking he'd discovered a clue to Isabelle and Maisy's whereabouts. The marshals service tailed him from state to state. When Seton reached Wyoming, Terry and I, from the Casper office, took over.

We stayed on him all the way here to your house. I understand you want to make sure Maisy is taken care of, but do you want more mercenaries showing up on your doorstep?"

Ms. Werth's gaze darted toward her porch, where muffled voices indicated EMTs and local police had arrived.

"Clearly, the answer is no. I don't want any more such visits." She returned her attention to Ethan. "Is that guy out there a mercenary?"

"Dolf Seton is half human bloodhound, if you want something or someone found, and half cold-blooded killer, if you don't care who dies during the search."

Ms. Werth cuddled the infant closer. "I know his intention was to scare me, but would the man really have killed me?"

"Seton would've killed you without a blink or a qualm if you'd stood between him and his objective. He probably would've shot you after he grabbed Maisy, simply to tie up loose ends. This is the sort of person Vincent Drayton has assigned to locate and seize his granddaughter. We believe now that his son is at large, Vincent intends to grab the child and flee the country with his family. Hopefully, we can continue to thwart his efforts and lure him and Ronnie out into the open and arrest them."

"You've got to be kidding me!" Ms. Werth gaped at him. "The baby is bait? I knew there was a motive deeper than protection somewhere in the mix."

"Not deeper." Ethan heaved a large sigh. "We absolutely want to keep the baby safe, but we also want to make the world safe from the Draytons and their gunrunning operation. They don't care who buys their weapons as long as they get paid."

"They sell to terrorists?"

Ethan nodded. "And Maisy won't truly be safe until they are put away."

Ms. Werth's gaze lowered toward the baby. "I do want her safe." The tone was thoughtful now, not adversarial. "But what she really deserves is to have her mother with her. Can you find Isabelle?" She directed a pleading expression toward Ethan.

That wide green-mixed-with-gold gaze ambushed him and melted a layer of the shield around his heart. The last time he'd let down his emotional guard on the job, people had almost died, including a child. Thankfully, everyone survived and the investigation had exonerated him of any fault. But he still won-dered if he'd allowed his judgment to be impaired by his affections. History was *not* going to repeat itself.

Ethan cleared his throat. "We'll certainly try. And not just the marshals service. Multiple law enforcement agencies are in on the manhunt. If you don't want Maisy in the care of a social worker, are you willing to come under marshals service protection with her? You probably should do that anyway. Even if we remove the child from your custody, the Draytons are likely to send someone after you to find out if you know where Izzy or Maisy are. The situation would not turn out well for you."

"I don't know. I—"

"Hey, Ethan!" Terry entered the room at a trot. The guy rarely did anything slowly. "I'm going to ride to the hospital with our suspect, make sure he gets his wound treated and then question him about the Draytons. You got everything under control in here?"

"Deputy Ridgeway was just explaining my options to me," Ms. Werth answered before Ethan could get a word out. "Nothing's been decided yet."

"Cute kid." Terry stepped forward and ran his finger under Maisy's chin. The baby chortled and kicked, sending milk bubbles down her little chin. "Ticklish, huh?" He grinned at Ms. Werth.

Lara answered with a dazzling smile that transformed her face from head-turning pretty to eat-your-heart-out gorgeous. Ethan mentally kicked himself for noticing.

"Ms. Werth and Maisy Drayton are under my protection," Ethan said, his tone a shade more forceful than he'd intended, and his reluctant hostess awarded him a cold stare.

"Sounds good," Terry said. "I'll see you at the safe house." Ethan's partner waved and loped out the door.

Ethan turned toward Ms. Werth. "I don't see that you have any options if you truly care about the safety of this baby and yourself."

The woman frowned. "I wish you weren't right, but I'm not one to cut off my nose to spite my face. Maisy's finished eating now." She popped the empty bottle from the infant's mouth. "I'll get her stuff and my go bag."

"You have a go bag?" Ethan's eyes widened.

She smirked at him. "I'm a nature-photography vlogger. I always keep a full backpack of travel essentials. You—" she waved a hand in his direction "—can get the infant carrier from the spare bedroom— Oh, no!"

"What?"

"We don't have the base for the car seat."

"There's a car seat piece that a baby carrier fits into sitting out on the porch. I noticed it when I kicked Seton's gun away."

"Observant." A mild grin crossed her face.

A spot of warmth formed under Ethan's breastbone. He squashed it. What did he care that she'd said something nice about him? This woman was his charge, and he was doing his job. Nothing more. Ethan gave himself another mental kick. Why was he even having this internal conversation?

Within a gratifyingly brief five minutes, they were headed out the door toward the deputy's vehicle. Going down the sidewalk, Ms. Werth sent a longing look over her shoulder at her house, but then pointed her face forward. Ethan wrestled the car seat into place in the back seat of his SUV, and Ms. Werth snapped the carrier into place.

"Easier than I thought it would be," she said. "I'll ride in the back with Maisy."

"Good idea." At least there wasn't going to be debate on *this* subject.

Ethan got behind the wheel and started the

vehicle. He pulled smoothly away from the curb and onto the quiet road of the modest but well-kept residential cul-de-sac. Ahead of them, from a busy cross street, a full-sized black sedan turned onto Ms. Werth's road and then a second one pulled up right beside the first, blocking the road. Ethan's heart formed a fist.

"Remember my question about not wanting more of Drayton's hired guns on your doorstep?"

"Of course," his charge answered.

"They're here."

TWO

"Do a U-turn," Lara blurted out.

"But we're in a cul-de-sac. There's no way out."

"I know a way." No time to second-guess herself now.

Deputy Marshal Ridgeway whipped the SUV around. He'd complied without further question? She could examine her astonishment at his lack of argument later.

"There!" She pointed toward a paved bike trail that led between two houses opposite hers on the street. "That trail leads out onto a through street."

Shouts came from behind them, commanding them to stop, but the deputy gave his vehicle gas and they lunged toward the slot between the houses. A gunshot reverberated, and Lara ducked, but there was no shattering of glass or ping of bullet against metal indicating they were hit. Another shot, but again there was no sign the bullet had done any damage.

The walls of the homes flashed past on either side of their SUV, and they broke into the open, straddling the slight dip that was the bike trail between the two backyards. With a jolt, they hopped the curb onto the street beyond. Horns honked as they darted into moderate traffic, but the deputy marshal performed a smooth right turn and merged into the flow.

"That was close," Lara said. "I'm amazed we weren't hit when those goons started shooting."

"They were trying to scare us into surrendering, not endanger the baby by actually hitting us. If they shot this kid they're assigned to abduct, the Draytons would shoot *them*."

"But that doesn't mean they won't kill you or me if they get the opportunity?"

"Now you're catching on."

"Where are we going? Vincent Drayton's people are in town looking for us, and now they know what you're driving."

"I don't dare head straight for the safe house. We'd just pull our enemies after us. Guide me to the police station. You and Maisy can be protected there until we can figure out a way to get you to a secret, secure location."

"Keep going straight on this road until I tell you to turn." Lara's stomach twisted. "How long will Maisy and I need to hide in this 'secret, secure location'? That's no way to live."

"Impossible to say, Ms. Werth, but we'll do our best to capture the Draytons as quickly as possible."

"Call me Lara. Now that we've been shot at and fled from gunmen together, it seems silly to stand on ceremony."

"Deal. And I'm Ethan. I'll be on your protection detail, so we could be spending a significant amount of time in each other's company."

Ethan got on his radio and notified the station they were coming while Lara settled back in her seat and checked on the baby. The little girl seemed unfazed by the wild activity. In fact, her eyes were drifting closed. Time for the morning nap, apparently. Smiling, Lara took one of Maisy's hands, and the infant curled her fist around Lara's pointer finger as her whole tiny body went limp in peaceful slumber. There went that warm, gooey effect the baby had on Lara's insides.

If things had worked out between her and

Matt, she might have her own baby by now. But then, marrying her ex-fiance would have been a horrible mistake, nearly on par with Izzy's choice of husband. Little Maisy, though, was a treasure nobody could regret.

Ethan said there hadn't been enough time for her to form an attachment, but this little one may as well have grabbed Lara by the heart as by the hand. Lara was a goner, and it was going to be a tremendous wrench when the time came to give Maisy back to her mother.

"You can turn left at this next stoplight," she told Ethan. "We're only about a mile from the police station now. Mostly a straight shot with one more right turn onto Pearl Avenue."

"Let's speed this up, shall we." Ethan flipped some switches, and the vehicle's sirens and lights came on.

Traffic ahead and around them moved aside as they roared up the road. Lara gripped her armrest tightly as they sped toward safety. Her gaze darted here and there, attempting to read the traffic for danger, but dark sedans were all over the place. It was impossible to tell which ones might contain enemies. They'd probably left their attackers behind, but being shot at tended to cause hypervigilance.

She didn't have Maisy's ability to simply relax and trust. Blithe confidence used to come easily, but that was before she'd invested her future in Matthew Sebring and found out how duplicitous and manipulative some human beings could be. That horrendous breakup, practically on the eve of the wedding, had left her with emotional scars as well as an aversion to any hint of being bossed around or controlled. Probably why her guard had gone up automatically against Ethan's overconfident assumptions about what she should do with Maisy.

Lara rubbed her thumb across the back of the baby's little hand. The skin was soft and smooth as warm butter. *God, please help. This little one deserves Your watchful care.*

"We're going to protect you," Lara whispered to the child. "You can trust us."

"We've got an escort," Ethan said as, halfway to their destination, a pair of marked police cars joined them. One took the lead position and the other pulled into formation at their rear.

At last they drove into the parking lot of the stone-fronted civic building, with its large round clocks on three sides of a short tower crowning the entrance. The officers emerged from their vehicles and escorted Ethan and her, carrying her go pack, the baby's bag and Maisy still sleeping in her carrier. Once through the doors, Ethan went into the bowels of the building with an officer. Another one guided Lara and Maisy to what must serve as a small conference room. Vague odors of scorched coffee and stale pastries tinged the air. Lara set the carrier on a table, took a seat and put her head in her hands.

She should probably call her mother and let her know what was going on, but she dreaded the difficult conversation. Mom would worry and fuss and feel helpless. But what if her mom was in danger, too? These people knew who Lara was, and clearly, they were determined and ruthless. Would they try to use her mother to get her to give up Maisy? Or was Lara being melodramatic from watching cop shows on television?

Lara lifted her head from her hands to find Ethan standing in front of her. An involuntary jerk flowed through her body. The man moved like a panther, stone quiet and loose-limbed. His blond hair was a slightly lighter shade than hers, and his eyes were more hazel brown than her hazel green with gold highlights.

Those piercing eyes studied her now. "Are you all right?"

"I'm worried about my mother."

The man pursed his lips. "Is she your closest relative?"

"Yes. My dad passed away nearly fifteen years ago. There are a few uncles, aunts and cousins, but we're not close with them. Too scattered all over the country."

"Good thinking about your mom. Where does she live, her place of work, that sort of thing?"

"Mom lives in Chicago. That's where I grew up—where I knew Isabelle from high school. My mother's name is Doris. She volunteers all over the place and organizes charity events. I can give you her home address and phone number and name a few of the charities where she donates her time. I have no idea what her schedule is today."

Lara gave Ethan the information, and he took note of it.

"I'll notify my office to locate her and put her in custody for the time being," he said with a nod.

Lara snorted. "I'll be impressed if you

can pull that off. She's a stubborn creature of habit and not likely to let her daily activities be disrupted by murderous thugs or officious deputies."

A smile lit Ethan's face, and it stripped away the businesslike air that he exuded. Lara dropped her gaze. No ring on his finger. That didn't mean he *wasn't* married, but it increased the probability of singleness. Of course, she couldn't allow his marital status to matter to her, especially when the guy was too good-looking for her peace of mind.

Not to mention forceful, smooth talking and turn-you-to-putty beguiling when he smiled. All part of the recipe that had sucked her in once before. Ethan didn't look anything like Matt, but their behavior traits were too similar for her to feel comfortable in his presence. Of course, Ethan *had* listened to her advice when they were escaping the cul-de-sac. Something Matt never would have done.

"Sounds like *my* mother," Ethan said. "Maybe you should call her first. Give her a heads-up. Want me to give you some space?"

"Please." Lara unzipped the pocket of her go bag that held her phone. She pulled out her cell as Ethan panther-prowled from the room. She dragged her eyes off his broad back and onto her phone. As she was about to tap the screen and initiate the call, a throat cleared from the vicinity of the doorway. Lara looked up.

A freckle-faced woman wearing a dark pantsuit and a serious expression stood in front of her. "Please come with me, ma'am. We have more comfortable accommodations arranged for you and the baby."

"I was just about to call my mother."

"You can call from there. It's not far."

With a mental grumble, Lara put her phone away, shouldered her go bag and picked up the baby's bag and carrier. The woman escorted her up a hallway, striding about half a step behind Lara. Something in the tension of the stranger's carriage raised the hairs at Lara's nape.

"Where are we going?" Lara began to slow her gait, but her escort crowded in close to her side and something hard poked her in the ribs. A gun? A shiver coursed down Lara's spine.

"Not a sound," the woman hissed. "Keep moving straight ahead."

A fair distance away stood a large metal door marked Exit. They passed a small office where a woman sat typing, her gaze riveted on her computer screen. They moved past another room where the door stood slightly ajar. Several voices carried to Lara, one of them Ethan's.

The gun jabbed her hard. "Not a peep!" her captor said in a tone of velvet-wrapped steel.

No doubt existed in Lara's mind that this woman would shoot her without a second thought. She was on her own against a killer who wanted to kidnap the baby in her charge. It would all be over for her if she allowed this woman to take them out of this building.

She had to *do* something. But what? She was no ninja fighter. Ah, but she *was* fit and fast from long hours of hiking and climbing to photograph and film her vlogs.

At her next step, Lara pretended to stumble forward. She released the baby bag and the carrier, which hit the floor with a small thump. Crouching and keeping herself between the gun and Maisy, she whirled her heavy go-bag toward her captor in one smooth motion. The woman cried out and her gun went off. Scrambling away, Lara lost her footing and hit the floor hard on her backside. She gaped up at the killer she'd struck with her pack. The woman's lips peeled back from her teeth in a snarl as she recovered from the blow and took aim straight at Lara's face.

* * *

The sound of a gunshot zinged an electrical charge through Ethan. Drawing his weapon, he raced into the hallway and pulled the trigger on the armed woman standing over Lara. Another shot echoed his own. The woman had fired, but she was already going down from being hit by Ethan's bullet. Her shot went wild, striking the light fixture above their heads.

"Lara, are you all right?" Ethan called.

"Maisy!" Lara cried out as she scrambled toward the car seat, where the startled baby had begun to wail. She unbuckled Maisy from the seat and gathered the infant into her arms.

A pair of officers crowded into the hallway and began to secure the woman Ethan had shot. Ethan skirted around them and reached Lara, who was seated on the floor, clutching the fussing baby.

"You're both all right?" he asked as he knelt beside them.

"Barely." Lara's voice was gulping and breathless, like she'd been running a marathon. "I couldn't let…that woman take us… out of here."

Ethan could hardly blame her for panicking. She was more than entitled after resisting an armed kidnapper at the risk of her own life. He leaned closer, patting Lara on the back and stroking the infant's downy head. The delicate floral scent of Lara's shampoo accented by the crispness of a woodsy soap graced his nostrils. Much like the woman herself, delicate on the outside but sturdy as an oak on the inside.

Pulling away from Lara and the baby, Ethan scowled toward the gunwoman. The would-be killer was cursing and moaning and clutching her bleeding leg as her weapon was stripped from her and she was cuffed.

"I want to know how this person got in here," he told the officers, "and I want to know yesterday."

At his bark, one of the officers jerked a nod toward him. "Right away, Deputy."

The other officer hauled the injured woman upright. "We'll escort her to the hospital for treatment and make sure she's kept secure."

"Do that." Ethan returned his attention to Lara and Maisy. "Jackson is becoming too hot. An informant notified us that the Draytons have put out a sizable reward for anyone able to bring them Maisy uninjured and—" He halted before completing the sentence. Lara was scared enough as it was. He could tell her the rest later, when they were in a secure location. "I would imagine all the greedy, ruthless pond scum in the area are converging on the town now. The small PD here isn't going to be able to handle the influx of hard cases."

Lara offered a somber nod as he helped her to her feet. "We need to get out of here." She bounced Maisy gently, and the child's whimpers subsided. "What is it you aren't telling me about the situation?"

Ethan released a soft groan. He might have known he wouldn't be able to hold back from this perceptive woman.

"Apparently, an official contract has been issued on your life. The Draytons don't want anyone left alive with a legal claim on Maisy."

"What?" Lara gasped. "How did they find out about the power of attorney assignment and what's in Izzy's will? I only discovered those documents this morning, and law enforcement found out shortly thereafter. Is there a leak in your department?"

Ethan shook his head. "We think it might be worse than that."

Lara's face washed pale. "The Draytons must have Izzy. She's the only one who could've told them about the authority she gave me. Do you think she's alive?"

"We don't know." Ethan closed his hand firmly around Lara's arm. "But we're going to keep you safe and keep Maisy out of the hands of ruthless criminals."

The depth and strength of his assertion sent a shock wave through him. Sure, he was doing his job, but this felt like…more. Not possible. He mentally shook himself. This couldn't be personal. He'd just met this woman. His duty was everything. That's all this was, and he would tell himself that until he believed it.

They walked up the hall and returned to the conference room.

"A marshals service helicopter is on its way to pick us up," he said. "While we wait, let me bring you something to drink. Water? Coffee?"

"Thank you. I could use some water." Lara's gaze dropped toward Maisy as the little girl started to cry and suck on her fist. "I'm hardly an expert on babies, but I think this little one is telling us it's time for her midmorning snack. Hold her while I mix up the bottle."

Before Ethan could think twice, Maisy was

in his arms. The little bundle squirmed and kicked. Her face puckered into a fierce scowl and turned red.

"It's nothing against you." Lara chuckled. "When a girl's hungry, she's hungry."

"I guess." Ethan smiled and bounced the baby.

Even throwing a fit, the child was adorable. This little one had her whole life before her. Who knew what great things she could become and do with the proper nurture and opportunities? No way could he allow her to be snatched and raised by criminal gunrunners, regardless of their biological kinship. If Isabelle Drayton was no longer alive, he'd seen enough of how Lara thought and operated to know that Maisy would be in good hands.

Their well-being was in *his* hands. He couldn't, wouldn't, fail them, especially by allowing emotion—specifically, this unwelcome attraction to Lara Werth—to interfere with his focus.

Finished with bottle preparation, Lara held out her arms for Maisy, and Ethan surrendered the child. Lara sat down in a nearby chair, gave the infant her bottle and in a split second, the tiny body went from rigid and squealing to relaxed and guzzling. Ethan smiled at the tender tableau—Lara with her blonde head bent over the infant while Maisy gazed back at her benefactor with big heart-stealing eyes.

"Ethan, buddy." Terry's voice yanked Ethan out of the very sort of emotionally charged contemplation he'd vowed only seconds ago to avoid when it came to Ms. Werth. Maybe he should go back to calling her that formal name simply to preserve proper distance—and his own sanity. He turned toward his partner.

"I heard what happened," his partner said, stepping farther into the room. "Glad to see everyone is okay. Seton is hospitalized under guard. I'm guessing the same will happen with the unidentified woman. Neither one is talking. Surprise. Surprise."

"I *won't* be surprised if we get a hit on the woman's identity when we run her prints. Someone with her ruthless savvy has been on the wrong side of the law for a long time and is likely to have a record. What I'm still wondering is how she got into the building."

Terry rolled his shoulders. "Chief Taylor of the local PD stopped me on my way back here and said she presented herself at the front desk as the insurance representative he was expecting this morning. Had a business card and everything. She knocked the real representative out cold in the parking lot, left the woman in her car and took the card. She successfully passed through the metal detector, and the dispatcher buzzed her in. As soon as she entered, she downed the guy with a plastic taser and took his gun."

"Resourceful." Lara summarized Ethan's inner reaction in a word. "Clearly, we're not dealing with mindless thugs."

"Don't worry," Terry said. "We're getting you and the baby out of here and to a safe location pronto. The chopper is landing as we speak."

"Are you ready?" Ethan asked Lara.

"Let Maisy finish her bottle. I also need to change her and then make that phone call to my mother. Oh, and I really could use that water."

"The phone call is out of the question," Ethan said. "No time. Let our agency secure your mother."

That familiar mulish look came over Lara's face. "But—"

Ethan held up a hand. "The situation has escalated, and the Draytons have the technological resources to tap your mother's phone.

We don't want to alert any listeners that she's being taken into custody before we have her in hand. In fact, I need you to give up your cell until this is over. As for the water, once we're in the chopper and away, we'll all hydrate."

"I might even be able to rustle up a few sandwiches for the journey." Terry chuckled and left the room.

Lara sniffed and scowled. "You know, you and your partner are a study in contrasts. Buttoned down versus hanging loose. Hydrate versus rustle up." Her sour expression smoothed as she busied herself changing the baby. "I'm sorry. That sounded critical, but it was more of an observation." She offered a small smile.

Ethan forced a return smile to cover the inner cringe. Was he really so stiff and formal? If he were truthful with himself, he'd have to agree with her assessment. By the book and distant was the persona he snapped in place when on duty. Too bad this woman seemed to have a knack for sneaking past his guard. He'd have to be more careful than ever from now on. In order to maintain a clear head to keep her alive and the baby safe, he needed to hold them at arm's length.

THREE

Even with the protection of her headphones, the helicopter's roar thrummed in Lara's ears. Through the side window, she peered down toward the ground as the chopper rose higher and higher. Her town of around ten thousand people was a map tableau beneath her. Was that her cul-de-sac—her house—growing tinier by the second?

How had her life changed so dramatically in less than a day? Suddenly, she was no longer the captain of her own destiny. She, and this little one in her care, were under the control of federal deputies.

Sipping from the water bottle she'd been handed as she boarded the chopper, Lara glanced at Ethan, seated across from her. The man's strong features inspired confidence even as they stirred unease. How much of her independence had she already forfeited to this commanding man she'd met only this morning? Her gaze dropped toward the gun strapped to his side along with other law enforcement paraphernalia on his belt. The sight ought to inspire comfort and confidence since he was her defense against people who were out to kill her, and to a degree it did. But part of her wanted to erect defensive walls against this man's Matt-like charisma and charm.

If Ethan thought she would obey his every order without question, he was wrong. She'd gotten the impression that her continual questions exasperated him, but he'd have to get used them. She was going to make lots of inquiries. And she'd think for herself, especially now that a little person depended on her.

Lara smiled toward the baby strapped into the helicopter seat beside her. The child was oblivious to the cute ridiculousness of the big set of ear protectors wrapped around her little head. Maisy seemed fascinated by her new environment. Thankfully, she didn't appear afraid, just curious.

"It's a great big world to figure out," Lara murmured to the child, though of course, Maisy couldn't hear her, much less understand her. Maybe she was talking as much to herself as to the baby.

With one hand, she deposited her empty water bottle in a holder attached to her seat. With the other, she reached into the go bag at her feet and pulled out her compact digital single-lens reflex camera. The small DSLR was handy for taking photos on the go. She snapped a few shots of Maisy. Then she turned and grabbed several photos of the city fading behind them and the rugged terrain below.

The city of Jackson sat in an elongated bowl of a valley known famously as Jackson Hole, nestled in the Teton Mountain Range. Of course, having a window between her and her photographic subject wasn't optimal, but the aerial shots were too rare to miss. Maybe when this was over, she could rent a chopper that would allow her to take photos with the windows open. A whole new vista of vlog subjects ran through her mind.

Her photography vlog had taken off with unexpectedly sturdy wings while she was in college, and now she worked from home in the house she'd inherited half a dozen years ago from her grandparents. Well, she didn't always work *in* her home. Her photo vlogs were set mostly in the magnificent outdoors, highlighting the flora and fauna of the mountains and lakes around Jackson. She did take the odd road trip to other sites of scenic interest.

She didn't answer to a boss, unless one counted the occasionally obtrusive expectations of advertisers on her site. If she made it through this crisis, she'd be thankful even for that annoyance, because it would mean she'd been able to return to a life she loved.

A big hand closed around her wrist. "What are you doing?" Ethan's voice echoed tinnily through her headset.

Lara rounded on him. "I'm sure you've seen cameras before, Deputy. This is what I do for a living."

He frowned at her. "We can't give our enemies any idea which way we're headed."

"Relax." She attempted to take her own advice and offered him a smile as nonchalant as she could muster. "I'm hardly going to upload these shots to the internet…at least not until this mess is well over."

He released her arm. "All right. If the activity keeps you calm and occupied."

She sniffed. "Patronizing much?"

"No offense intended." He lifted a hand, palm out.

"None taken." *Yeah, right!* If steam could

come out her ears, her headset would be smoking.

As they flew north across the National Elk Refuge and Grand Teton National Park, Lara recognized landmarks and snapped photos right along. Then the chopper veered eastward. They weren't headed into Yellowstone National Park, then. The green pine and gray rock vistas before them began ever so gradually to smooth out into foothills rather than jagged mountain peaks.

From a seat kitty-corner to Lara, Ethan's partner rummaged in a large paper sack and pulled out wrapped sandwiches and small bottles of water. He asked her which kind of sandwich she preferred, and Lara accepted her lunch with a grateful thank-you. She'd barely swallowed the last bite of her pastrami on rye when Maisy began to fuss.

Lara studied the child. She shouldn't be hungry yet, and she'd been changed before they took off, so…bored maybe? Lara began to entertain the baby with her camera, helping the little girl feel all the different buttons and gadgets but not allowing her to suck on them. Maisy quieted and even began to coo and blow little bubbles with her dainty lips.

Perhaps a future photographer? *Adorable* was an inadequate term.

A warm chuckle sounded in Lara's headset, and she glanced toward Ethan. He was watching the baby and her play together, an unaccustomed softness in his eyes and around his mouth. Maybe this deputy marshal wasn't such a Mr. Macho-in-Charge after all. Or maybe he was all that and more, too. Lara's heart did an unwelcome little jig. If he turned out to have a tender side and a sense of humor, she was in real trouble. Best she continue to think of him as a stranger behind a badge.

He was also the guy who'd saved her life with his gun—twice now. She had to give him that.

They passed over several small towns scattered far apart, and dense forestation yielded to pasture and farmland. At last, the helicopter began to descend toward a small airstrip that appeared to be located in the middle of nowhere, but that Lara guessed might be near the town of Cody. They set down with a minor bump, and a pair of armed men flanked the door. One of them opened it and nodded toward Ethan.

"Let's get out," he said. "Our hideaway has been prepared."

He descended from the helicopter, the still-whirling rotor blades barely rustling his short-cropped hair. Lara unbuckled Maisy's car seat and passed the child in her carrier to Ethan's waiting arms. Terry offered Lara his hand as she moved toward the door, but she declined with a smile and hopped out without assistance. Her shoulder-length hair went wild beneath the rotor blades. Good thing a quality brush was an item she kept in her go bag.

Ethan motioned her to follow him as he headed toward a black van that sat on the tarmac with its engine running. They were quickly and efficiently on the road, with Terry riding shotgun and Ethan and Lara behind, the baby situated between them. A sizable escort car went ahead of them and one behind.

"I'm feeling positively presidential," Lara said with a little laugh.

Ethan smiled. "Don't get used to it. Once we arrive at our destination, you'll only see Terry and me. Everyone else will melt into the environment, but there will be sentries watching."

"Good to know." Lara nodded.

Within an hour, they had reentered a forested area, and shortly thereafter, the escort vehicles pulled over onto the side of the road and allowed Lara's vehicle to proceed without them. Almost immediately, the van turned onto what looked like a little-used track that wound here and there, apparently at random. They jounced a bit over uneven terrain, and the trees—mostly pine—crowded in close to both sides of the large vehicle. Suddenly, they popped out into a large clearing. Ahead of them was a medium-sized A-frame house with a large porch. A small detached garage sat next to the house, and a county sheriff's car was parked in front of the garage door.

"Temporary home sweet home." Ethan motioned toward the dwelling as the driver brought the vehicle to a halt.

"This is a place the marshals service maintains for witness protection?" Lara asked.

"Something of a way station for people entering WITSEC. But WITSEC is permanent relocation and identity reassignment, not your status at this time, and I hope it never comes to that. Our intention is to return you to your regular life as soon as you and Maisy are safe from the Draytons."

"Which means you need to successfully

apprehend them. What can I do to help make that happen?"

Ethan's gaze intensified, and Lara's skin prickled beneath the assessing stare.

"Pray," he said, "and stay alive and take care of Maisy."

"Things that are already on my list of priorities," she told him.

In the front passenger seat, Terry turned his head toward them. He was frowning. "Wonder where the advance team of local law enforcement is. They're supposed to step out of the house and let us know everything is secure."

"I'm wondering the same thing," Ethan said. "I'm going to check it out." One hand went toward the door handle and the other to his gun.

"No, me." Terry waved. "Your door opens toward the house with no cover for you if hostiles are waiting inside. You stay with Lara and Maisy."

Lara's pulse throbbed in her neck. They'd left an unsafe situation at the police station in the town where she lived, and now they were in the boonies where no one was supposed to know their location, and something was wrong already?

In smooth movements, Terry drew his gun and left the vehicle. Lara glanced from one member of her protection detail to another. Not comforting that both the driver—a serious-faced young woman—and Ethan had also drawn their guns.

"Hello in the house!" Terry called, keeping the van between himself and the building.

There was no response. Terry turned and exchanged glances through the window with Ethan.

"Call it in." Ethan tapped the driver on the shoulder. "Tell them to get those escort vehicles back here for us. We're leaving."

Maisy started to fuss, and Lara patted the child's little arm. Perhaps the baby sensed the tension in the air. More likely, she needed to be changed. Which wasn't going to happen soon if they had to flee this site.

"Get in!" Ethan called to his partner.

Terry turned toward the van just as a roar split the air, and the house disintegrated into a blossom of vivid red, orange and yellow. The explosion rocked the vehicle, throwing Lara's body against her door panel and banging her head against the window. Pain ratcheted down her side.

A shot rang out from the forest, and Terry

dropped from sight. Ethan sprang from the vehicle in a low crouch, weapon extended.

"Go! Get out of here!" he hollered to the driver.

The vehicle lunged forward in a hiss of spinning tires, and Lara threw herself across a howling Maisy. More gunshots rang out, though none pinged against the van's sides. Ethan must be the target—and Terry, if he was still alive. The driver put the vehicle into a sliding one-eighty and then barreled up the narrow track. Lara's breathing stuttered as she sat up and stared through the rear window.

Terry lay in the clearing on the ground, unmoving, but Ethan stood tall, gun blazing—selflessly providing an opportunity for the driver to get Maisy and her away. Any second now, he would go down beside his partner. Her heart tore.

Something with the strength of a mule kicked Ethan in the chest and slammed him to the ground, driving every molecule of oxygen from his lungs. Pain splintered through his torso. His throat rasped as he struggled for air. Suddenly, his lungs filled, and he lay drinking in smoke-tinged air as if it were the elixir of life—which it was. The darkness edging his vision receded, and he forced himself to rise up on one elbow.

Nothing except the wind stirred in the trees. No one emerged from the forest seeking to finish the deputies off. Had the gunman vacated the area after flushing Lara and the baby away from the supposedly secure house?

His gaze flew to his partner, who barely stirred on the ground. Blood coated the man's upper right arm. Ethan crawled toward Terry.

"Hey, buddy," Ethan said. His partner's eyes squinted open. "You hit anywhere other than the arm?"

Terry groaned. "Took one near the heart, but the vest under my shirt must have stopped it or we wouldn't be having this conversation." He groaned again. "Probably have a broken rib or two, but I'm not going to die anytime soon. You okay?"

"Similar to you, but without the arm wound."

Ethan sat up and used a zip tie from his belt pouch to form a tourniquet on the profusely bleeding arm.

"I need to call this in." He whipped out his

phone. "I hope those escort cars pick up the van before Drayton's people do."

A gunshot blasted from the direction the van had disappeared. Ethan sprang to his feet, pistol at the ready.

"I'll call. You go!" Terry cried even as Ethan raced toward the sounds of distress.

Ignoring the complaints from bruised or broken ribs, Ethan pelted up the narrow rutted track. If anything happened to Lara or Maisy, he'd never forgive himself. The US Marshals Service had been entrusted with their care. It was up to him to ensure such trust was not misplaced. Surely, duty was the only reason his heart was clogging his throat.

From a short way ahead, just around a bend shielded by a thick stand of trees, a woman screamed. Ethan heard the baby crying and a masculine voice snarl a curse.

"Just shoot her and let's get out of here," said another male.

Ethan put on another burst of speed and rounded the tree line. A short burly man had Lara shoved up against the side of the van with one stiff arm. The other arm was lifting a gun toward her head. Ethan fired instantly, and the gunman dropped like a stone and lay moaning and rocking on the grass, clutching his knee. Lara shrieked the baby's name and pointed toward a second man, who dangled Maisy's car carrier from one hand and held a gun in the other.

"Drop the weapon!" Ethan ordered as he took up a solid shooter's stance. The man who held the fussing baby glanced toward him, then Lara, then back to Ethan again, mouth slightly agape.

"I'm not inclined toward mercy at the moment." Ethan's tone emerged as a lethal growl.

The man's weapon thumped to the ground. With a cry, Lara charged forward, wrested the baby carrier from the gunman's grip and retreated to the far side of the van.

"Are you all right?" Ethan called to Lara.

"I'm fine. Just shaken up."

He sent up a mental prayer of thanks. As he secured the would-be baby snatcher, Lara's gentle murmurs to the child carried to his ears. Maisy's crying receded and then stopped.

Ethan assessed the scene. The man he'd shot—the one who'd been about to shoot Lara—was still groaning on the ground. Ethan quickly secured him, also. The guy would need to get to a hospital, but he wasn't bleeding out. A spike strip lay across the track directly behind the van, indicating why the vehicle had stopped with four flat tires. The windshield sported a starred bullet hole, and the driver lay slumped against the steering wheel.

Ethan sucked in a breath. He shoved his uninjured prisoner into the back seat of the van, then opened the front door and felt for a pulse in the driver's neck. It was there, faint but steady. *Thank You, Lord.* Heat bubbled in his gut. A vest didn't protect anyone from a head-shot, but the bullet must have only grazed the driver, knocking her out. They were going to need emergency services pronto, though. Terry should have already called for those.

Ethan leaned in toward the man in the back seat. "Any more of you near here?"

"Just you wait." The guy sneered at him. "An army is on the way."

"How did you know about this safe house?"

His captive shrugged. "Got a phone call telling us where to go, what to do. Apparently, me and Bill were the closest assets to the location."

Ethan snorted. "You talk like you're employed by some sort of legitimate intelligence outfit rather than a thug working for cockroach weapons dealers. What did you do with the county sheriff's deputies who were supposed to be waiting for us inside the house?"

"We're here," said a woman's voice behind him.

Ethan turned to find a pair of uniforms walking toward him—a male and a female. A pale-faced Terry trailed in their wake. Lara came around the van and stood beside Ethan. Her strained features and the white-knuckled grip she maintained on the car carrier told him fear still wrapped her in its fist. Sensible person. The danger was far from over. He resisted the impulse to put an arm around her shoulders and pull her close.

"How did you survive?" Lara gazed up at him with wide eyes.

He offered her a smile, hoping the gesture held more assurance than he felt about their situation. "I'm wearing a concealable bullet-proof vest. It's protocol to wear one when on protection detail."

Her lips trembled into a faint smile. "Good protocol."

"We were ambushed," said the male deputy as the trio reached Ethan and Lara. "Knocked out cold, tied up and locked in a storage shed out back. Your partner found and freed us."

The man jerked a nod toward Terry, who stood swaying on his feet.

"I need to get Lara and the baby out of here," Ethan said to his partner. "The suspect in custody says more of his people are on the way."

"For sure." Terry nodded. "But I just got off the phone with headquarters. Our prior escorts have reported in. Their vehicles met with a similar fate as the van. They're out of commission."

"Then I need to take Lara and Maisy in whatever vehicle these goons arrived in. It's got to be around here someplace. I'll disable the GPS to ensure we can't be tracked."

"I think it's right there." Lara pointed toward a shadowy opening in the trees a dozen or so feet up the track, where a large object was covered by camouflaging branches.

From this location, it was just possible to make out the slightly unnatural lines of the object beneath the branches. From the direction of the road the small clearing was all but invisible.

"Sharp eye." Ethan gave her a nod and turned toward his partner and the two sheriff's deputies. "Between possible concussions and a gunshot wound, all of you need medical attention. Help should be coming soon, but Lara, Maisy and I can't wait around to see who arrives first—the good guys or the bad guys."

"We've got this," said the female sheriff's deputy. "Leave the suspects in our custody."

"And we'll give any crooks who arrive before the cavalry a warm welcome." The male marshal patted his sidearm.

"What they said." Terry's grin wobbled, and he staggered slightly where he stood.

Ethan stepped forward and helped his partner to a seat on the ground, leaning him against the side of the crippled van. The intensity in Terry's dark eyes snagged Ethan's attention.

"There's something you ought to know, buddy," his partner said. "I talked to Marshal Teague himself. The service is compromised."

Ethan's heart lurched. "A mole?"

Terry shook his head. "One of our top computer techs, Alex Bingham, has been kidnapped. They think the Draytons have him and they're squeezing him for every bit of knowledge that will help them snatch the baby."

"That's how they knew about this safe

house. Bingham would have been able to access those location records."

"You got it. Marshal Teague says we've revoked our guy's server access, but we're still scrambling to discover how much damage has already been done. We don't know what the Draytons might know about our safe sites and protocols."

Ethan's jaw muscles went rigid. "I have to take our charges completely off-grid, then. Away from any known marshals service connections."

The man nodded, face waxing a deeper gray. "You're on your own, but if anyone can navigate a safe way out in the cold, you're the guy. We'll work on catching the Draytons." Terry's left hand closed around Ethan's right. "You keep Lara and Maisy safe."

Ethan squeezed his friend's hand and then released it. He rose and faced Lara. She gazed back at him. If he'd ever seen grave determination on a human face, he was seeing it now.

"I heard." She lifted her chin. "Maisy can count on us—you and me."

Ethan nodded, his respect for Lara climbing another notch. "Let's go."

The sheriff's deputies cleared the camouflage from the gunmen's midsize sedan while

Ethan and Lara collected their bags and Maisy's belongings from the van. The keys had been left in the sedan's ignition—a typical precaution for someone who might need to make a quick getaway.

Since their enemies had a skilled computer technician in their possession, Ethan took a few moments to disable the GPS on the car so the system couldn't be accessed and their location couldn't be revealed. He also removed the battery from his cell phone. Since the agency's database had been hacked, their enemies could have his private government number and use his phone to find them. They might not have his number, but it wasn't a risk he was prepared to take.

Soon, he had the vehicle out on the highway, moving westward at a pace just under the speed limit. He and his charges were now cut off from any help from the marshals service. But that didn't mean he couldn't accept aid from another branch of law enforcement. Ethan knew just the place they could go to ground—provided they could get there before their pursuers caught up with them.

FOUR

Lara gnawed the inside of her cheek as she held a hastily prepared bottle in Maisy's mouth with one hand and gripped the armrest on the car door with the other. Sparsely forested scenery flew past her back-seat window as they sped south at a westerly angle. The terrain had begun to climb steadily in elevation. Evidently, they were returning to the mountains.

"Where are you taking us?" she asked Ethan.

"I have a friend with a ranch nestled in the Wind River Range."

"How are they going to feel about us bringing trouble in their direction?"

Ethan's broad shoulders rippled in a shrug. "Rogan's a DEA agent, so danger is no stranger in his line of work. Trina's a veterinarian, real gutsy woman. If they were home, they'd stand shoulder to shoulder with us against anything the Draytons could throw our way. But Rogan and Trina left five days ago for a veterinary convention in Minnesota. After that, they're taking a summer vacation canoeing the legendary Boundary Waters along the Canadian border. The couple is incommunicado by now, deep in the wilderness, but Rogan and I have a *mi casa es su casa* friendship. They'd be the first to say come on over and make yourselves at home, so we will."

An involuntary sigh slipped between Lara's lips. How had life suddenly blown up into such a mess that they were reduced to lying low like squatters in someone else's home? But their options were severely limited, and if Mr. Competence deemed this place safe and their welcome assured, she'd go along with the plan. For Maisy's sake more than her own.

The baby had finished the bottle, and her eyes were drifting closed. At least someone was relaxed and content. The child had no concept of the danger that crept around them, waiting to pounce, or that her mother was missing.

Where was Izzy? How was she faring?

Was she even alive? Lara's stomach turned and she shifted in her seat.

"Try to get comfortable, maybe even grab a nap." Ethan's tone was gentle—soothing, even. "It will be a long drive."

"Let me know if I can spell you behind the wheel," she answered.

He chuckled. "And potentially leave me helpless in the face of baby tears?"

"You'd figure it out." She smirked at the back of his head.

"I appreciate the vote of confidence, but I don't yet have a wife and kids I'm clueless."

Lara scolded her rebellious heart for doing a little skip at the confirmation this man was single and, even better, the word "yet" indicated openness to the possibility of changing that situation. Neither his marital status nor his hopes for a future family had anything to do with her, and she needed to keep that assertion in the forefront of her mind.

"Plus, I'm an only child," he went on, "so I never had any experience looking after siblings or even the possibility of infant nieces or nephews."

"Ditto," Lara said. "And my part-time high school job was photographer's helper in a neighborhood shop, so I never babysat. My first exposure to infant care was this morning. Izzy left written instructions, I followed them and voilà, Maisy gets fed and changed."

"Photographer's helper. Is that how your interest in photography began?"

"Without that job, I might never have known I have a knack."

"Funny how life goes sometimes. You said you're a nature vlogger? How does a Chicago native get connected with the great outdoors?"

"That part happened my freshman year in college." Lara smiled. Those memories were precious. "My boyfriend at the time was an avid wilderness hiker and started dragging me along to state and federal parks to traipse through the woods, up hill and down dale. I brought my camera along and found out I loved the outdoors and taking pictures of nature and wildlife. That interest outlasted the boyfriend. Pretty soon, I was casually vlogging my adventures, and it turned out, much to my pleasant surprise, people liked my photos and my little essays and poems about them."

"A creative career was born." Ethan chuckled.

Was she mistaken or did Ethan's tone hold

a note of admiration? Warmth spread through her chest. Why did she care what the deputy marshal thought about her or her occupation? But apparently, she did care, and the unwelcome fact raised red flags in her head.

Desire for approval had tangled her up in a disastrous relationship once before. *Caution, girlfriend, caution.* There was no room for personal feelings under direly dangerous circumstances. Too bad the guy was terminally cute and not such a tyrant once one caught on that his take-charge personality was well-intentioned rather than scheming and manipulative as Matt's had been.

"Shall I turn on the radio?" Ethan asked. "What kind of music do you like?"

"Contemporary Christian."

"Another thing we have in common." He began flipping stations.

"You're a believer?"

"A follower of Jesus? That's a resounding yes. What I do exposes me to a lot of the darkness in people, and things don't always turn out for the best. I can't see how anyone—especially someone in my line of work—can get through life without faith that God is real and justice will ultimately be served."

Lara's heart leaped. Everything he said resonated with her, especially that thing about ultimate justice. She opened her mouth to tell him so, but the words froze on her tongue as Ethan's station surfing brought up a news broadcast.

"The hunt for escaped felon Ronald Drayton has come to Wyoming," said the male commentator, "since the discovery this afternoon of his badly injured, estranged wife in a Cheyenne motel room. Undisclosed evidence indicates that people answering to Drayton are responsible for her injuries and that the convict himself may even be in state. Isabelle Drayton was taken to Cheyenne Regional Hospital, but Drayton remains at large."

A deep moan escaped Lara's chest. *Poor Isabelle.* What a wrenching situation for her to be hurt and hospitalized, as well as separated from her child.

"At least Izzy's alive," she said to Ethan. "I'll be praying for her full recovery."

Lara glanced down at the sleeping baby. The child's feathery eyelashes cast small shadows on plump cheeks, and the little bow of a mouth made tiny sucking motions as she slept. Lara's heart wobbled. Yes, she dearly wanted her friend to survive and regain her health, but that meant she'd have to give Maisy back to her mother. Of course, that was the best thing all around, wasn't it?

Lara's head said yes but her heart ached. She might see little or nothing of the child once Izzy took Maisy and went back to her life in Chicago. Lara's livelihood depended on easy access to wilderness locations, so returning to city life was out of the question, even if she wanted to resume urban living—which she didn't. From any angle Lara looked at it, the parting would be bitterly hard, so she might as well start preparing herself for it. But how did one carve a child out of one's heart once she was embedded there? The answer was simple. One didn't.

A weight settled in the bottom of Lara's stomach. What was best for Maisy was her mother. Any pain Lara might feel in the transition didn't matter. End of story.

The stony silence ringing from the man behind the wheel abruptly caught her attention.

"You're glad they've found Izzy alive, aren't you?" she asked.

A long breath huffed from Ethan. "Yes, I'm glad she's been found."

The words were gentle and affirming, but the tone was cautious, even secretive, as if he were holding something back. She'd heard that tone from him before when he hadn't wanted to tell her about the contract the Draytons had put out on her life. Realization struck her, and her head spun.

"You think information is being kept back. That Izzy might not have made it, but the public isn't allowed to know she's gone. If Ronnie or his father hear the news that she's in the hospital, they might return to finish the job and be caught. She's bait. Just like Maisy and I are."

Ethan turned his head slightly in her direction. "I don't *know* that's the case with Isabelle, but I don't want you to get your hopes up about your friend and then have them dashed."

Lara's gut curdled. She'd needed this reminder that she was a pawn in a bigger game. If she kept that truth squarely in the forefront of her thoughts, she'd have proper ammunition to battle this foolish attraction to Deputy Marshal Ethan Ridgeway. He was nothing to her other than the man tasked with protecting her and Maisy, all while he tried to harpoon the sharks swimming after them.

Ethan rubbed the aching spot on his chest where the bullet had struck him just under his heart. "I'm sorry," he said. "I know this is a harsh situation for you. Hopefully, it will be over soon. As much as I dearly wish I could offer more reassurance about Isabelle, I can't make any promises. You're a good friend to her, you know. You're certainly going well beyond the extra mile to keep that baby safe. Rest assured, I will do the same thing for you both."

What effect his encouraging speech had on Lara, he couldn't tell, because she was sitting directly behind him and he couldn't see her face. This was one of those times he could use a pair of eyes in the back of his head. She had his deep respect already for the way she'd been handling herself. A lot of people would be panicking, but she rolled with the punches and came back swinging—sometimes literally, as the bruise on the arm of a certain hitman on her porch could attest.

"I appreciate the multiple times you've risked your life on our behalf," she said, her voice tinged with the weariness that the ebb of adrenaline brought about. "Thank you."

"You're very welcome. I was just doing my job. How is Maisy?"

"Sleeping."

"Good. I'd like to keep driving until she

wakes up. Then we can pop briefly into a convenience store in the nearest town. We'll need to get gas, and we can take care of our needs and grab some food and beverages."

"Sounds like a plan. I think I'll take your advice to try and take a nap until then."

The sudden blare of an unfamiliar ringtone raised the hairs on the nape of Ethan's neck. The noise seemed to be coming from inside the center console. He pulled the vehicle over onto the side of the road, under the cover of a copse of pine trees, and lifted the console lid. A compact burner phone stared back at him. The screen was lit with an unfamiliar number.

"Are you going to answer it?" Lara's voice quavered. "It could be Vincent or Ronald Drayton checking on the status of their abduction squad."

"Or it could be a middleman seeking the same answers. But, yes, I'm going to answer it and hope to coax some info from whoever it is."

Ethan lifted the receiver to his ear. "Hello."

Stone silence answered.

"You're not one of mine," a harsh voice suddenly blurted. "Who is this?"

"Deputy Marshal Ridgeway. Not who you

were expecting?" He laced his tone with acidic ice.

A guttural curse singed his ear in response from the caller. "Why aren't you dead yet? Just wait, you—"

The furious rant was cut off and silence fell.

"What my son means—" a cool voice ended the pause in conversation "—is that this can all be over in a moment. Give us his daughter—*my* granddaughter—and we will go away. In fact, we will leave the country and be no problem again. Simple as that."

Ethan barked a laugh. "You know it's not that easy. Ronnie needs to go back to prison and you need to join him. Tell us where you are, and we'll pick you up. *Then* it will be over."

The older man snorted. "Allow me to speak to Maisy's guardian." Vincent's tone had turned impatient.

"Not going to happen."

"Then expect us when you least expect us. We *are* going to take custody of our own."

The call went dead.

"They're still coming after us," Lara said, voice flat.

"You know it, but now I have a cell number

to pass on to my colleagues. It's a long shot, because I'd be surprised if Vincent didn't discard his phone as soon as the call ended, but we can't assume so. Pinging or running GPS on the number might help us get a fix on these crooks' location. Or at least where they were as of a minute ago. I'll call Terry on this burner phone and then toss it so no one can track us through it. We left your cell at the Jackson police station. I still have mine, but it's turned off and the battery has been removed."

"Then we can't be found via cellular service?"

"Correct."

"Okay, but please ask Terry if my mother is safe."

"Consider it done." Ethan punched Terry's number into the burner phone, and it rang several times. "Come on, buddy, pick up."

At last, a familiar voice muttered a cautious hello.

"Terry, where are you? Are you okay?"

"Ethan!" The man's tone sharpened. "I didn't recognize the number."

"Burner phone in the car. Belonged to our perps."

"Yeah, I'm okay. The ambulance just arrived, as well as a state highway patrol car. We're good. You?"

"Fine, but I just got done talking to both Draytons on this phone. I'll send you the number they called from."

"I'll have our people see if they can get a location."

"Good. Lara is understandably on pins and needles about the status of her mother. Can you check on that? I'll hang on to this phone until you get back to me."

"On it."

The call ended and silent minutes passed. But finally, the burner ringtone sounded, startling a gasp from Lara.

He pressed the speakerphone button on the burner. "What did you find out?" he asked his partner.

"Not much." Terry sighed. "Mrs. Werth wasn't present when local officers arrived at her condo to take her into custody, but there was no sign of intrusion or any kind of altercation. We're hoping she's simply out on errands or gone for some other reason. The officers are sitting in their vehicle across the street, waiting and watching for her return. Ask Lara if she knows where her mother might be."

A rustle sounded from the back seat, indicating Lara leaning forward. "Check at May's Beauty Salon or with her friend Salina Gray. She was our neighbor when I was a child. Mom talks to her almost every day. I'm sure you've tried calling my mother's phone. Isn't she answering?"

"Negative."

"That's the way my mother is." The exclamation communicated equal parts disgust and desperation. "I can't believe how she doesn't pick up when it doesn't suit her."

Ethan grinned into the rearview mirror. "I take it your mom is not one of those folks enslaved to her cell."

"I used to think that was a good thing." Lara huffed. "But right now, it's maddening."

"Agreed." He returned his attention to the phone. "Terry, if you're up to it, keep tabs on the hunt for Mrs. Werth. We'll be in contact later when we can, but I'm going to get rid of this phone since the number is known to the Draytons, and they could use it to locate us."

"Understood. Next time you call me, route through the main office in Virginia. They'll connect you to the new number we're all being issued. We're not sure how many of our phones are compromised since that security breach."

"Will do." Ethan ended the call, powered down his side window and flung the phone into the trees.

"We'd better get back on the road," he told his passenger.

"Sure." Her tone was heavy. "But I doubt if I'll be able to sleep now."

He didn't blame her for feeling discouraged and probably worried about her mother.

"We'll find her," Ethan said.

He put the car in gear and backed out onto the deserted county road. If only he could be certain his words were true.

They drove for a full hour and then Maisy began to fuss, so Ethan started looking for a place to stop for gas and essentials. A few minutes later, they cruised into a tiny one-convenience-store town nestled in the surrounding pine forest. Ethan pulled the vehicle up to one of only two pumps.

"I'm going to take Maisy to the bathroom and change her," Lara announced.

"Do that," Ethan said as he stepped outside into warm air laden with the odor of gasoline and juniper from nearby trees. "I'll fill the tank and 'rustle up' some grub, as Terry might say."

Lara chuckled as she exited the car. Her laugh was a light, pleasant sound he'd not heard from her before, and his spirits lifted. They were completely off-grid, so it might not be too much to hope for a nice respite from being chased and shot at. His lovely charge disappeared into the small but well-kept store with a wiggling baby in one arm and diaper bag dangling from the other. For someone with no experience in childcare, the woman was a natural. His heart warmed.

What would it be like to be a dad with a brave, attractive and intelligent wife like Lara? Would he ever get the opportunity to find out? Correction. More like, would he ever *allow* himself the opportunity to find out? This was certainly not the time, place or situation to be having these thoughts. But then when was? Thus far, his job had been his world. The US Marshals Service came with demanding responsibilities he'd embraced wholeheartedly and inherent risk he'd willingly accepted. Maybe when this was over, he'd take a little time to reassess where his life was headed.

God, are You trying to tell me something?

He hadn't felt such restlessness about his single-minded career focus since—well, ever. Not even when that guard detail went sideways years ago. He cringed internally as he remembered the incident. Totally different situation. There'd been no romance involved, just an unwise investment of trust where it hadn't been deserved. His faith in his own judgment of character had sustained a major hit that had required a long time to rebuild.

Firming his jaw, Ethan put the gas nozzle back where it belonged and closed the cap on the car. Gaze roaming the surroundings, he crossed the distance between the vehicle and the front door of the convenience store. He'd pay cash for this transaction, not only because the ancient pump in this tiny burg wasn't equipped to accept credit cards, but because he couldn't afford to leave an electronic record of their stop here.

A bell over the door jingled as he walked through, but that wasn't the sound that drove his heart into his throat. A screech of tires outside yanked him into a crouching whirl. A black SUV came to a rocking halt on the far side of the vehicle he'd just filled with gas. Three men and a woman, all dressed in dark clothing, lunged out of the SUV, weapons drawn.

How had they been found?

Again.

FIVE

Lara sang softly to little Maisy as the child lay on the changing table and cooed back at her. The baby's lively kicking and wriggling had made the diaper-change process a bit of a challenge, but at last, Lara finished fastening the tape.

"There you go." She guided Maisy's plump little legs back into her lightweight sleeper.

Sudden hammering on the door sent a pang through Lara's middle.

"We've got to go. Now!" Ethan's urgent growl skyrocketed her pulse.

Lara snatched up the baby, snagged the diaper bag, then opened the bathroom door. Ethan stood outside, grim-faced and gun drawn. He ushered her and her precious cargo up the narrow hallway at the back of the store where the bathrooms were located.

A wide-eyed, pale-faced young man stood at the emergency exit. It was the store attendant.

"Go!" Ethan whispered.

The youth jerked a nod and shoved open the door, admitting a rush of pine-laden air. The young man darted outside ahead of them in a full-on run into the woods behind the building. Ethan's warm hand pressed between Lara's shoulder blades had her hurrying after the attendant. She bit her lip against a rush of questions and yielded to the pressure even as a strange man's voice from the front of the store called out their names and ordered them to come forward.

Her feet grew wings. She hugged Maisy close and charged for cover in the trees. A masculine shout came from behind her. Not Ethan. Then a gunshot, with another loud report close on its heels. Enemy fire followed by Ethan's response?

There was no time to spare a backward glance. She plunged into the woods, twigs snapping beneath her feet and pine needles raking her body. Ahead, the young attendant seemed to know where he was going as he dodged around trees and leaped fallen logs. Lara scurried in his wake.

But where was Ethan?

More gunshots sounded behind her. The deputy marshal was holding off the attackers, giving her and Maisy and the innocent bystander the best possible opportunity to escape. She yearned to help Ethan, but she couldn't. Getting the baby to safety was the priority and the task fell to her. Besides, she wasn't armed.

Gunfire rang out again. Lara winced and jerked with every shot, even as her feet flew faster on the heels of the whimpering and huffing store attendant. Another gun blast, and a pained cry sounded in the distance behind her. Ethan? *God, please no!* A bitter, metallic tang filled Lara's mouth. So this was what terror tasted like.

Ethan ducked behind a set of rusting barrels that hugged the rear wall of the gas station. One adversary was down, lying still on the grass outside the rear exit, but the situation was still three to one, and he was running out of ammunition. An arm reached out the door and took another shot at him. The bullet pinged off one of the barrels. Ethan crouched lower, sparing a glance over his shoulder toward the corner of the building.

Whoever was taking potshots at him from

the rear exit was no doubt the distraction meant to keep him focused in one direction, but Ethan wasn't dense enough to think the others weren't even now coming around the store, trying to sneak up behind him. He needed to move out quickly before he was taking fire from two directions. There wasn't much help for it. He'd have to sprint for the woods a few long yards away.

Sucking in a deep breath, Ethan sprang from cover and sent a pair of shots in the direction of the rear exit. Then he ducked and rolled toward the tree line even as an adversary zinged bullets into the spot where his torso had just been. Ethan was still wearing his concealed vest, so taking a bullet in the chest was unlikely to kill him outright, but allowing impact to slam him to the ground would turn him into a sitting duck and ensure his demise.

The woods embraced him. He sprang to his feet and lunged behind a fat trunk as a pair of bullets *thwacked* into the wood. He peered out and returned fire on the two figures—one male, one female—rushing toward his location from around the corner of the store building. As he had expected, they'd been trying to flank him.

Ethan sent a bullet followed by another in their direction. They both went down but quickly rolled in opposite directions—one darting behind the barrels that had recently sheltered him and the other lunging behind a knot of bushes. Apparently, he'd only winged them, but at least wounds would slow them down.

He was out of ammo now. Flight remained his only slim option to survive.

"Where...are...we going?" Lara gasped at the store attendant as she caught up to him.

The young man had slowed considerably from his original high-speed sprint, and the wheeze in his breathing didn't sound good. Digging in his jeans pocket, the youth abruptly halted and slumped against a tree trunk. His hand emerged from the pocket with an asthma inhaler, which he stuffed into his mouth. A couple puffs later, normal color returned to the teenager's face.

"S-sorry." He bent over, coughed and then straightened. "I...had to stop."

"No problem." Lara struggled to control her breathing while bouncing a fussing and obviously frightened Maisy. "Do...we have a...destination in mind?"

"Who were those people with guns?" The store attendant cast wide eyes in the direction of his workplace.

"Thugs hired to kidnap this baby."

The attendant scowled, gaze hardening. "Talk about lowlifes!"

"Exactly."

"I'm Bryan, by the way."

"Lara." She stuck out a hand and Bryan squeezed it. "If you've got your cell on you, maybe you should call the local authorities for help."

The young man snorted. "What local authorities? The nearest cop shop is half an hour away. Besides, I left my cell on the counter in the store."

"Never mind." Lara's heart fell. "Let's keep going."

"The deputy marshal showed me his badge when he ordered me to go out the back way, so I know you're the good guys." He turned and started down a barely discernable path between the trees. "Follow me. I'll take you to where we can score some wheels."

Lara cast a glance over her shoulder as she stepped out behind her young escort. Where was Ethan? The gunshots had ceased. Did that mean Ethan was dead? Her gut twisted.

Was she now on her own against the powerful Drayton juggernaut?

Ethan crept deeper into the woods, keeping to the cover of trees and bushes as much as possible. Stealth, not speed, was his best ally now. Drayton's hired guns would certainly follow them into the forest, and their priority would be catching up to Lara and the baby. He needed to be able to hear the enemy's location without betraying his own and take advantage of any opportunity to ambush their pursuit.

A snapping twig, a thud and a muttered curse let Ethan know one adversary had stumbled about eight yards to the south of him. He froze in position, straining his ears for more sounds and his eyes for signs of movement. There! A figure stepped along, lifting his feet high and gazing around as if the trees were about to pounce on him. Good. Wilderness was clearly not this guy's comfort zone.

Ethan eased himself in the man's direction, stalking the thug, waiting for the best moment to take him by surprise. At his feet, a short but thick fallen branch presented itself as a possible club. Ethan scooped it up. Not-too-distant rustles in the foliage betrayed the locations of the other two hired guns—no doubt searching for clues to the direction Lara and the baby had gone. But Ethan maintained his course, intent on dealing with one goon at a time and possibly snagging a firearm.

"Over here!" a female voice called.

The thug Ethan was tracking grunted and abruptly changed direction, heading straight for Ethan. He stepped behind a tree, holding his makeshift club at the ready. The man blundered past him, gun and gaze swiveling this way and that but completely missing Ethan's presence. Ethan swung his club like a bat at the guy's head, and the thug dropped like a stone. The man was still breathing but unconscious. With zip ties from his utility belt, Ethan secured the hired hitter, helped himself to the extra ammo clip the man carried and scooped up the guy's weapon.

Ethan moved on soundlessly in the direction of the snap-crackle-pop noises the remaining two adversaries were making as they hurried toward their quarry—Lara and Maisy. Ethan pressed his lips together and narrowed his eyes. They didn't know it, but now the hunters were the hunted.

* * *

Thankfully, Maisy had stopped crying and settled into Lara's arms, gazing here and there with interest at her surroundings. Then Lara tripped over a fallen branch and nearly fell, startling a squawk from the baby.

"This way!" came a shout from an unfamiliar voice. "I heard them."

Lara's throat tightened. The outcry sounded far too close to their location for comfort.

Her teenage escort gripped Lara's arm and pulled her along. "Just a quarter mile to my uncle's place. We can call the cops and you can borrow a vehicle."

"We'll never make it."

Bryan's lips thinned. "It's the cave, then."

"The what?"

He didn't answer as he plunged deeper into the forest. Lara followed willy-nilly. Soon, they came to a moderately steep cliff side.

"We're trapped," Lara whispered, sending a wide-eyed gaze over her shoulder. Their pursuers could come upon them any second.

"Watch this." The teenager grinned at her, then crouched and leaped into the air.

His hands caught and held on to an outcropping of rock. He half pulled, half scrambled up the cliff side and onto the lip of what must be a ledge, though the width of it wasn't visible from the ground. From her perspective, there shouldn't be room enough for a human body atop the outcropping, but obviously, perception from this angle was faulty.

Lying on his stomach, Bryan reached down toward her. "Give me the baby."

Lara's grip tightened around Maisy. Hand her little charge to someone else? Nearly unthinkable. Thrashing and snapping noises from not too far away in the woods made her decision for her. She thrust Maisy up toward the youth's reaching arms. The infant, along with all trace of Bryan, disappeared over the side of the lip. Lara's heart did a little *kabump*.

"Come on up." The teenager's voice trickled softly down to her.

Lara jumped up and wrapped her fingers around the edge of the rocky lip. A little scrambling later, and she hauled herself up onto a ledge that formed the floor of a horizontal crevice leading into the side of the cliff. No wonder it looked from below as if the cliff side proceeded upward in an unbroken line.

A soft baby mewl drew Lara deeper into the crevice on her belly. Shortly, the narrow opening grew into a larger space where she could sit up. Light filtered dimly into the area, and she found Bryan nearby, sitting cross-legged and bouncing Maisy in his arms.

The whites of his teeth gleamed briefly in her direction. "Every kid in the area knows about this cave, but if you're a stranger, you'll never find it."

"I can believe that." Lara hauled in a deep, calming breath, and her pulse rate began to slow. "I'm worried about Ethan, though."

"The guy acted like he knew what he was doing, but all that shooting going on back there didn't sound good."

Gunfire sounded on the heels of Bryan's words. Goose bumps erupted on Lara's arms. Ethan? He must still be alive and active down there in the woods.

"I've got to take a peek."

She rolled onto her stomach and inched through the crevice. Her hand fell upon a hefty rock and her fingers curled around it. Lara reached the cliff's edge, keeping her head and body flat against the rock beneath her. Her gaze searched the perimeter. Ethan! Her heart leaped. He was taking cover behind a tree, but behind him crept a burly man lifting his gun and taking aim at the deputy marshal.

* * *

Ethan glided into cover behind a tree trunk. One more bad guy—er, bad girl—was down and trussed up. But that left one adversary standing. And he didn't know the location of the fourth one who had been sent after them. However, the guy had a good approximation of *his* location because of the shot he'd just taken.

Scarcely daring to breathe, Ethan went stock-still except for his head swiveling this way and that. A cliff blocked the way in one direction, but the dense forest offered many places for his enemy to hide. A worm of sweat inched its way down his nape and into the collar of his shirt. Behind him, a guttural grunt and a thud brought him into a whirling crouch, gun extended. The last gunman lay facedown in a nest of pine needles, not twenty feet from him. What had happened?

"I got him." Lara's voice came from the cliff above.

Ethan turned and looked up. Lara waved to him from a seat on what appeared to be a dangerously narrow ledge.

"How did you do that from there? You're not armed."

She grinned and shrugged. "I had a bird's-eye view, and there's plenty of rocks up here. Never underestimate the arm of the starting pitcher for a high school softball team."

A pent-up breath gushed from Ethan's lungs. "No, I guess I won't make *that* mistake. Let me secure the perp, and then I'll help you climb down." He went over to the sprawled gunman, squatted down and checked the man's pulse. The guy seemed fine, just out cold. He began making good use of more zip ties. "Where's Maisy and that store clerk?" he asked with his eyes on his task.

"We're here and we're fine," Lara said from a spot a few feet away.

Ethan jerked his head up to find her approaching him with the baby in her arms and the store clerk strolling in her wake. Electric warmth rushed through his muscles. Lara and Maisy were all right. Everyone was all right. *Thank You, God.*

Without a second thought, he opened his arms and Lara rushed into them. Pine needles were strewn in her hair, and their crisp scent filled his nostrils. She fit perfectly against him, even with the baby making a threesome.

"I thought you might have been killed." Her words came out muffled against his shirt.

His insides clenched. What was he doing,

holding the woman he was protecting? It was one thing to offer comfort after a terrifying experience and quite another to be enjoying the closeness. *Professional distance, buddy.* With an effort, he released her and stepped away. A hint of confusion passed over her face at his abrupt backing off, but then her expression went blank.

"Not dead yet," Ethan said. "Thanks to your pitching ability." He looked toward the young convenience-store attendant. "Thank you for looking after Lara and Maisy."

"My pleasure." The kid grinned. "Most excitement we've had around here in—like, ever."

"This is Bryan," Lara introduced the youth. "His knowledge of the local cave pretty much saved the day."

"Along with your shooting." Bryan nodded toward the gun in Ethan's holster.

Ethan looked down at the groaning thug, who was starting to wake up. "I need to round up the other living perps. Then we'll head back to the store. Bryan, why don't you hustle on ahead and give local law enforcement a call to meet us there. And tell them to bring the county coroner," he added with a grimace.

He could only be thankful that the latter

official wasn't being called on behalf of Lara or Bryan. Bullets had flown around the vicinity of a child because the Draytons had pulled out all the stops to grab her. Ethan's teeth ground together. Ronald and his father, Vincent, took evil to the next level.

Within ten minutes, their group had reached the store. Bryan showed Lara into the break room, where she could feed the baby, who had begun her hungry fuss. Ethan watched them disappear into the back room. Funny how he'd already started to know what Maisy wanted simply by the way she cried. Was that a normal thing, or was he getting way too attached?

Ethan shook off the alarming thought with a ripple of his shoulders and herded his captives toward the store office, where he secured them to scuffed wooden chairs. The two men and one woman glared at him as he relieved them of everything in their pockets, especially their burner cell phones. He scanned through their call records and found nothing to indicate they had reached out to anyone when they'd found their quarry at the store, offering hope that no reinforcements were on the way.

Ethan allowed himself a deep breath and

stared at them. "How about someone clue me in on how you found us?"

The trio's jaws firmed, and they pressed their lips together in mirror images of stubbornness.

"What can it hurt to answer the question?" Ethan crossed his arms over his chest. "It's not like I'm asking you to reveal your bosses' location."

One of the thugs sneered up at him. "We were driving past and spotted our pals' car. Figured it had to be you."

Ethan's gaze clashed with the man's stare. The thug looked away first and squirmed in his wooden seat. Something about the answer didn't sit well, like information was missing from the story. Yet an accidental sighting was plausible if the Draytons had as many troops out hunting for Maisy as the marshals service suspected. But the answer had been too glibly and almost sarcastically forthcoming.

The female hireling snorted. "Don't bother asking us where the boss and his son are. We don't know."

Ethan bottled a sigh. It seemed likely these hired killers didn't know where Ronnie and Vinnie were located. These hired killers' ignorance of Ronnie and Vinnie's location seemed all too likely to be true. Still, he might as well continue questioning them. Maybe they knew something they didn't know they knew.

Twenty minutes later, the county sheriff and a deputy marshal arrived, accompanied by the coroner. Ethan left the thugs in the care of the local authorities. He went to the break room and found Lara with Maisy on her shoulder, patting the child's back. The empty bottle on the table said that Maisy's appetite had not been affected by the recent excitement. He offered Lara a smile.

She looked up at him, gaze shadowed. "Did you find out anything from our attackers?"

"According to them, finding us was a bit of a case of right time, right place."

"Will we be getting more company soon?"

"I hope not. There's no record in their phones that they reported our location. But we shouldn't stick around any longer than necessary."

"Agreed."

"Before we leave, I need to use the landline to call Terry."

Lara gathered the baby's things and trailed him to the office. The sheriff, deputy and coroner were still around processing the scene.

They had taken the captured suspects to a squad car, so he and Lara, with little Maisy, were alone in the small room. Lara took a seat on one of the wooden chairs and began entertaining the child with a plastic toy key ring from the diaper bag.

Ethan got on the store's phone and called Terry via the Virginia headquarters office.

"It's me," Ethan said when his partner picked up. "How are you doing?"

"Pretty well. I've been discharged from the hospital, and I'm at home cleaning up and changing."

"Any update on tracking down the Draytons?"

"We still don't have a clue to their location, but our computer tech was found staggering down a county road in the middle of nowhere, ten miles outside Cheyenne."

"Has he been able to offer us any good intel on his captors?"

"He was given an overdose of ketamine and was completely incoherent when he was found. Since then, he's lapsed into a coma and is in the ICU. It's touch and go for him."

"Sorry to hear it." Ethan groaned. "For him and for all of us. Lara, Maisy and I just survived another attack."

A sharp intake of breath sounded on the other end. "You need to go to ground quickly in a safe place. Being on the road gives our enemies an opportunity to spot you."

"We found that out all right." Ethan's tone was wry. "We're leaving shortly, and I'm going to arrange for another vehicle—one not known by the hired guns hunting us."

"Smart."

Lara's eager nod at him confirmed she agreed with his plan.

"We'll get some of our people out there as quickly as we can," Terry said. "We need to squeeze those perps for every shred of information."

"I did some squeezing myself," Ethan said. "They were acting cagey about something. Maybe you can find out what it is, but we won't be here when you arrive. I'll get back in touch with you whenever and however I can."

Lara nudged Ethan. "Any news about my mother?"

"I heard that," Terry said. "Negative. She's still MIA, but we're beating the bushes."

Ethan took the phone away from his ear and gazed down at Lara. "No sign of her. Is it unusual for your mother to be out and about all day long?"

She frowned and her brow furrowed. "I wouldn't say it's unusual, but under the circumstances, it's worrisome."

"Agreed," Ethan said and brought the phone back to his ear. "What about Isabelle Drayton? The news report said she'd been found in a hotel room. Is that true?"

Terry's deep sigh in response didn't bode well, and Ethan darted a glance toward Lara. She perched on the edge of her seat with her gaze riveted on him.

"Mrs. Drayton was found in Cheyenne, badly beaten," Terry said. "She was in the hospital in what appeared to be a coma, but now she's disappeared. Took off on her own, apparently."

"She what?" Ethan scrunched his brow. "How did she evade the protection detail stationed outside her door?"

Lara's mouth opened with what must be a flood of questions, but Ethan held out a quieting finger and she subsided.

"What can I say?" Terry grunted. "The woman is clever."

"Are you sure she wasn't kidnapped by the Draytons?"

"I doubt kidnappers would take the time to

dress her in her street clothes prior to whisking her away."

"Good point. Hang on a sec." Ethan lowered the handset and turned his gaze toward Lara. "Isabelle slipped her protection detail and is in the wind again."

Lara hugged little Maisy. "At least this child's mother is alive for real. Poor Izzy. She's probably more afraid of her husband and his father than she is confident that your people can protect her."

Ethan frowned and nodded. He'd had bitter experience with that kind of thinking before. He returned the receiver to his mouth.

"I'm back," he told Terry. "Anything else to report?"

"Not much." His partner's tone was dark. "All law enforcement personnel throughout the state are looking for Mrs. Drayton and Mrs. Werth."

"I'm sure you're leaving no stone unturned, but all of that hunting would be moot if we could lay our hands on the Draytons."

"No kidding." His partner snorted. "I hope to have good news to share when we speak again."

"I'll leave you to it, then."

Ethan ended the call. Lara's face had gone white and worry lines etched her forehead.

He knelt in front of her and clasped one of her hands in his. "We *will* find your mother."

She squeezed his palm, then pulled her hand away. "I know your people will do their best, but how do we know my mother isn't in enemy hands already?"

"Because no demands have been made."

"That's true." She inhaled a deep breath and let it out slowly as color returned to her face. "I'm okay now. What else did Terry have to say?"

Ethan rose and quickly updated Lara on what Terry had told him about finding the computer tech and the man's current condition.

She bit her lower lip and looked away, blinking rapidly. "I'm glad your partner's all right, but that's terrible about your tech guy. So many people are getting hurt."

Ethan's heart warmed. This woman might be tough, but she had a compassionate soul.

He placed a hand on her shoulder. "I'm going to arrange with the sheriff for a fresh set of wheels."

He needed to take Lara and Maisy and put as much distance between this location and them as possible. If Vince Drayton's people were monitoring statewide police-band radios, they would know a gunfight had occurred at this convenience store. That information would be enough for them to send people over to investigate. The next wave of attackers could arrive at any time.

SIX

On the road again.

The thought limped across Lara's mind as she gazed out the rear passenger-side window of the club-cab pickup the sheriff had arranged for them to borrow. They'd also taken a few hasty minutes to grab sandwiches to gobble on the journey, as well as some supplies to meet Maisy's needs and groceries to tide them over once they reached their destination. It was important they stay put and not show themselves until this crisis was over.

They'd been driving for almost an hour, and the highway was winding upward along a steep mountainside. Lush valleys spread out below them, skirted by another tree-belted mountain beyond. Beams from the late-afternoon sun glinted over the sparkling-blue water of a boulder-strewn river leaping and dancing through the wedge of the valley below. Normally, she'd be drinking in the view with a photographer's eye, but today, the dramatic vista barely stirred her senses.

Her nerves were stretched tight as piano wire, and it didn't help that Maisy was fussy. She glanced over at her little charge, who was mewling unhappily and waving her fists in the air. Maisy had been fed, changed, burped and played with, but she didn't seem inclined to fall asleep. Maybe she sensed the tension in the adults in the truck, or perhaps the child was simply bored from being stuck in a vehicle for so long today. The driving was getting tedious for Lara, as well, but it beat being used for target practice.

She could use a friendly hug right now—like the caring one Ethan gave her back in the woods when she was so shaken up after the attack at the convenience store. She'd felt completely safe. For about five seconds. But then he'd suddenly pulled away with that stiff mask of his firmly snapped into place. She'd hoped the impersonal persona had gone away for good.

Not that she expected romance from him. Of course not! Completely inappropriate. She understood that. But what about after this mess was over? Lara shifted in her seat.

What was the matter with her? Overwrought emotions were playing havoc with her brain.

"You're quiet back there," Ethan said.

"It's been a long, tiring day." Lara sighed, shoving uncomfortable thoughts away.

"I can't argue with that and I'm sorry."

"You have nothing to be sorry about. You've risked your life repeatedly for Maisy and me, and I'm grateful. I just want all this to end. For life to get back to normal. But a part of me understands that normal will never be what it was pre-Maisy. The feeling is… unsettling."

"Life sometimes throws us into situations that turn everything upside down."

Something in Ethan's tone hinted he was talking about himself as much as her, but prying into his life didn't seem necessary or right. They didn't know each other like that.

"Don't get me wrong." She leaned toward Ethan. "I don't regret for a second opening my door to my friend and her baby in their time of need. Izzy thought she was bringing Maisy to a safe place. I'm sad she was wrong."

"I'm *happy* I was wrong about the newscast being used as some sort of decoy for the

Draytons, and that Isabelle is actually among the living."

"Me, too, but her behavior puzzles me. Why flee the people trying to protect her?"

"I'm baffled, as well. But hopefully, we'll have answers soon, and the Draytons will be in custody."

"I hope so, too, but I turned in my rose-colored glasses a long time ago."

"I'm not going to ask." He glanced over his shoulder at her.

"It's okay. You don't have to ask. I'll tell. It's no secret." Maybe if she ever needed to ask *him* something personal, he would be as forthcoming as she was about to be, but she wasn't going to hold her breath. He seemed pretty closed off.

"Eight years ago," she said, "when I was fresh out of college, my fiancé and I had a fierce row. I told him I'd decided to let my best friend bake our wedding cake, like she'd offered to do as a gift to us. But he insisted we stick with the fancy and expensive bakery cake that would impress his co-workers. I stood my ground because I was certain my friend would do a wonderful job on the cake, and I refused to hurt her feelings by turning her down. He couldn't handle me not starry-eyed and compliant, so he dumped me less than a week before our wedding."

"Wow! Sounds petty of him. I'm sorry about that."

She let out a small laugh. "It was a long time ago. I was devastated in the moment, but it turned out to be the best thing that could have happened. In twenty-twenty hindsight, I now see what kind of man he was and how I had allowed him to manipulate and control me. Today's not the first time I've dodged bullets. Not winding up married to him was a big dodge for me, and the experience left me cautious."

"Understandable, and not entirely a bad thing—well, except for the bad experience you had to go through."

"I'm stronger and wiser—I hope—because of it, but my mother is starting to think I've given up dating altogether. She has grandchild fever, and I've been too busy building my vlog readership to make time for a family."

"Until one got dumped on your doorstep. At least temporarily."

Lara looked down at Maisy, who had gone quiet, to discover the little girl sleeping peacefully. She cupped one of the infant's little hands in hers. Something deeply maternal had now been stirred in Lara's heart. She wasn't going to be able to hide behind her camera any longer when it came to getting serious about finding love and starting a family. However, there was no forcing love. Who knew when she'd meet the right one?

Her gaze flew to Ethan's strong and handsome profile. She blinked and looked away. Not now, of course, and certainly not with a guy who was officially her hero. It would be too easy to mistake intense gratitude for something deeper and more lasting. She couldn't afford to get it wrong again. And she couldn't afford to even be thinking this way at this place and time. What was the matter with her?

"We're almost there." Ethan interrupted Lara's musing. "Forty-five minutes, maybe. We're skirting Shoshone National Forest near the Wind River Mountain Range."

"I recognize the area of the state. I did some popular vlog posts from a hike I did along the Continental Divide National Scenic Trail that goes right through this area. The views are beyond gorgeous. It's part of a trail system that extends from Canada to Mexico, which was a fascinating factoid for my followers. I hope to experience more of the trail and vlog about it—well, whenever I'm able to get back to my work."

"Sounds like a fun hike. I've never tried it, but you've piqued my interest. When I get the opportunity, I'm going to look up this vlog of yours."

"Thanks."

Warmth settled around her heart. Why did she care that she'd snared the interest of this man? Well, other than another potential follower for her vlog. Who was she fooling? She never went gooey like this when others indicated interest in her work. She experienced satisfaction, yes, but not the warm fuzzies. Yet she had to remember the situation they were in was extreme. That must explain the extreme reaction.

Probably.

Maybe.

Not long later, they came to a building site with a long, low ranch house, a big barn, a horse stable and a small shed. The sign beside the driveway advertised trail rides and riding and roping lessons, courtesy of Jim and Amy Miller, owners of Wind River Stables. Ethan turned the car toward the house. They glided past a corral, where a man with graying hair was grooming a horse.

"This is your friends' place? I thought you said they were on vacation."

"No, this is my friends' friends' place. They have the keys for my friends' place."

Lara laughed. "That was a mouthful of an explanation."

They pulled up near the front stoop of the farmhouse, and a plump middle-aged woman stepped outside, wiping her hands on a checkered dish towel.

Lara looked toward Ethan, and he smiled over his shoulder at her. "Let's get out. I'll introduce you to Amy."

The baby chose that moment to start fussing.

"You go greet your friends' friend," Lara said, "while I get Maisy out of her seat."

"Do that. Amy will gush over that cute little kid."

A few minutes later, Lara found herself seated at a plain rectangular table in a simple wooden chair in a kitchen decorated country casual, feeling welcome and completely at home. Apparently, Maisy shared that sensation of welcome, and she kicked and cooed while Amy cradled her and spoke in the sing-song way people did with babies.

The ranch woman smiled toward Lara. "She's adorable."

"She is that." Ethan chuckled while pouring himself a cup of coffee from the pot on the counter.

Lara bottled a smile. Evidently, Ethan considered himself right at home here, too.

"You've known Ethan for a while, then?" Lara asked.

Amy glanced at the deputy. "We met him the day before our friends Trina and Rogan got married. My husband, Jim, had the privilege of giving Trina away during the service because Trina's daddy passed away a while back."

"And I was Rogan's best man," Ethan put in.

Amy sat down across from Lara. "We met around this very table to discuss the last-minute details before driving to town for the rehearsal."

Ethan waved his mug at Lara. "Everyone invited into Amy and Jim's house is treated like family. Would you like a cup of coffee?"

Lara looked toward Amy. "Do you have any tea?"

"Of course, dear." The older woman rose and handed Maisy to Lara. "Coming right up. I'll make that tea while you—" she sent a sharp look toward Ethan "—tell me what brings you here."

"While you're making the tea, I should change Maisy." Lara stood up, bouncing the little girl, who'd started to fuss mildly.

"Go right ahead, dear. The bathroom is up the hall and to your left. It's got a spacious counter."

Lara started in the direction Amy had indicated and then stopped and turned toward Ethan. "Call Terry, would you, and check on the status with my mom?"

"You got it." He nodded.

The mellow tone of his voice filling Amy in on their situation followed Lara down the hall. Five minutes later, she returned to the kitchen with a dry and happy Maisy to find Ethan alone and talking on the landline. The call to Terry, no doubt. She stepped forward, pulse jumping. Had they found her mother yet and taken her to safety?

Ethan cradled the phone and turned toward Lara. His gaze was shadowed and his lips turned down. Her heart squeezed in on itself.

"It's your mom," he said.

* * *

The terrified expression on Lara's face tore Ethan's insides.

"She's been kidnapped?" Lara burst out.

"No, she's hurt. Our people located her coming out of one of those places where she volunteers, mere moments before a group of thugs in ski masks attempted to grab her. Gunfire was exchanged, and the marshals service managed to secure her, but she was hit in the cross fire."

Lara's eyes grew wide and she clapped a hand over her mouth.

Ethan approached and laid his hands on her shoulders. "It's not as bad as it sounds. Your mom is in satisfactory condition and recovering in the hospital, under heavy guard by deputy marshals and officers from the local PD. We won't allow Drayton's goons to get close to her again, and I doubt she has any plans to slip away from her protection detail."

"This is all my fault." Lara backed away from him, gaze wild. "I should be there. I need to be there. She must be so scared."

"Hang in there!" Ethan lifted his hands, palms out. "First off, *none* of this is your fault. Second, your presence at the hospital would increase the risk factor to her and others exponentially."

"How is that?"

"If the Draytons get a whiff that you're in Chicago, their base of operations, they can literally mobilize an army to deal with you, not merely these scattered carloads of attackers. They won't care who they gun down to take you out of the picture and get to Maisy, because once they have her, it sounds like they plan on pulling up stakes and fleeing the country. They have nothing to lose and everything to gain. Is that what you want?"

Cuddling Maisy close, Lara sank onto a kitchen chair. Silent seconds ticked past as she sat staring at the laminate floor. Then she lifted her head and met Ethan's gaze.

"No, becoming a danger to others, particularly my own mother, is not what I want to do. So, what's the plan?"

Ethan sat down across from her. "First off, give Maisy to me for a bit." Frowning mildly, Lara allowed him to take the little girl. She was a warm lapful who kicked her legs and cooed up at him. He smiled down at the tiny heart-stealer then looked up at Lara. "Now, drink your tea. It will help settle you."

Lara sniffed slightly but complied by taking a sip of the hot brew, but her grip on the mug showed white knuckles. If only he could express to Lara in words how deeply he understood the difficulty of this situation, but words would sound hollow. All he could do was continue to keep her and Maisy safe.

"The plan is the same as it always was," he said. "Go to ground in a safe haven. Right now, that means my friends' ranch a short drive from here."

"But what hope is there of this ordeal coming to an end anytime soon?" Lara bounced Maisy on her knees and won a happy chortle from the baby.

At least someone in this room was in a good mood. Ethan pasted a smile on his face and tickled the child's little neck.

"You're good with her." Lara's return smile shared the strain in his.

"Thanks," he said. "Never thought I'd be good with kids."

"Why is that?"

A pang struck him. How could he explain to her the incident from years ago that had nearly cost him his career and his sanity? What would she think of him then? Truly, it wasn't something he could talk about with her right now—probably never.

He offered her a smile and a shake of his head. "The situation isn't hopeless, you know. Far from it. The marshals service took into custody a couple of those thugs who attacked your mom. Our best interrogators are grilling them now. Let's give them time to do their jobs."

"Okay, then." She nodded. "We should probably get back on the road."

"Let's say goodbye to Amy, then. Jim is with the horses, so maybe we'll get a wave out of him as we head for Rogan and Trina's place."

The drive to their ranch haven was silent, except for audible sighs periodically released by his adult passenger. Lara's thoughts must be all over the place, and he could understand why. Her life had taken a radical turn. She'd gone from having a successful, adventurous career to living a moment-by-moment existence with mortal danger at every turn. She was the walking, talking embodiment of the saying "what a difference a day makes." But in the negative.

If only he could make the end of her day better. They'd packed the truck with groceries from the convenience store, so he could prepare her a tasty meal, see if he could get her to relax and rest tonight. But he couldn't take away her legitimate concerns about her mother's well-being or Isabelle's or the baby's or even her own. Their lives were all on the line until the Draytons were brought to justice.

"This is a really nice place." Lara's words drew Ethan out of his dark thoughts as he drove the truck into the lush valley that cupped his friends' rural homestead.

A long, low ranch house with a full-length porch dominated the center of the valley. Attached to the home by a narrow covered run was a smaller building with a sign over its door that advertised Trina's veterinary clinic. A machine shed sat to the side and away from the house and clinic complex, and there was a large red barn with adjoining corral on the other side of the house. Artfully placed shrubbery and colorful flower beds edged all the buildings, and healthy, beautiful trees were scattered over the grassy acreage.

Ethan pulled the truck to a stop near the front door of the house. "Wait here. I'll get out and make sure we're alone."

A soft groan from Lara hinted she was reliving vivid memories of the last time they'd pulled up to a supposed place of refuge. Visions of explosive mayhem were also attacking his brain, but he wasn't about to let on to Lara about nagging thoughts. This place looked completely buttoned down, the way it should look with the owners gone and all the animals staying at Jim and Amy's place, but he was taking no risks with his precious charges.

Ethan stepped out of the vehicle into the warm evening air laden with a variety of appealing woodsy and floral scents. Birdcalls met his ears, a good sign that goons with guns might not be lurking around the property, waiting to ambush them. But he had to make certain. A reasonably quick walk-through of the property reassured him.

He opened Lara's pickup door. "Come on out. All clear."

She turned toward him with a slight smile. "That's a relief."

"It is, isn't it?" He grinned at her.

Maybe this was going to turn out to be a safe place to lie low. They could all certainly use a break from the constant attacks.

Lara released the infant seat from the car carrier and handed the child to him. He accepted charge of little Maisy and stood aside while she grabbed the diaper bag and her go bag and got out.

She paused, gazing around the area. "This is so picturesque. I could do a great vlog episode set right here."

"Maybe after this is all over, Rogan and Trina will agree to the photo session."

"That would be great." She offered him a full-blown smile. "It feels good to think about something other than this trouble swirling around us."

They went into the house, and Lara made appreciative comments about the tastefully rustic interior decor.

Ethan set the baby seat on the sturdy wooden coffee table in front of a large leather sofa. "I'll start carrying in the groceries."

"You do that while I get Maisy squared away. I'm sure she'll be delighted to get out of that infant seat and maybe have some tummy time on a blanket on the floor."

"Go for it."

Keeping his eyes and ears open for any hint of trouble, he grabbed a few grocery bags from the bed of the truck and returned to the house. Lara was already on the floor with Maisy, but her attention wasn't on the little girl. Her frowning gaze was focused on a rattle she held in her hand.

She waved the item in the air and made a frustrated noise in her throat. "This toy is defective. Why does this rattle not rattle?" She wagged the toy in the air again, and sure enough, it gave no sound.

"Let me have a look." He deposited the grocery bags on the coffee table next to the infant seat and accepted the item from her.

Ethan sat down on the sofa, turning the object over and over in his hands. No sound came from within. The toy was made of heavy-duty plastic designed to withstand a baby's teething habits. It had a long thick handle and a large orb on the end. He didn't know much about baby toys, but presumably, the orb was intended to be hollow and contain smaller objects that would create the rattling sound when the handle was shaken. Clearly, the toy was broken or—he took a closer look—had been tampered with.

He pulled his folding knife from his pocket and sliced through a glued seam that held the orb together. With a wrench, he broke the toy open. A rectangular black object lay jammed into the hollow of the orb.

Chills raced up and down Ethan's spine. A

GPS tracking device. So much for their safe haven. Their enemies likely had a read on exactly where they were.

SEVEN

"What is it?" Lara jumped to her feet and stepped over to where Ethan sat. She sucked in a breath. That rectangular object embedded in the toy didn't bode well. "Tracking device?"

"Looks like it to me." Ethan's words came out clipped as if his vocal cords were strung tight. He pulled the device apart and removed the tiny battery. "Not transmitting any longer."

"But we still need to get out of here." Lara began stuffing items into the diaper bag. "They might already be on the way."

"I wish you weren't right about that." Ethan scooped up Maisy and planted a kiss on the child's forehead.

Despite the scary situation, Lara's heart warmed at Ethan's spontaneous display of affection. Not that it would be any of her business, but he'd make a great daddy one day, paired up with a happy woman. If they survived this danger. She prayed he would get the opportunity—and that she would one day be a mom, also.

He handed the baby to her. "Get her buckled in while I hurry up and call Amy and Jim on the landline to let them know we've been tracked and to watch out for potential hostile visitors."

Lara's stomach clenched. How she hated that others were put in danger because of their situation. Wordlessly, she nodded and got Maisy ready to go while Ethan made the call. He was fast about it and soon they were headed out the door—she with the baby and the diaper bag and he with her go-bag and the groceries. Wherever they went, they were going to need provisions. They trooped back out to the truck. Lara scanned the road for any approaching vehicles. None in sight yet. So far, so good.

The tires spurted gravel as they tore away from the ranch. A giant fist squeezed Lara's chest as she looked over her shoulder for pursuers. The road remained empty as the home of Ethan's friends faded in their rearview mirror.

At last, Lara faced forward and allowed

herself a full breath. "How did our enemies plant that device in the diaper bag?"

"Good question." Ethan's tone was dark. "We found evidence someone had been in Isabelle's Chicago apartment. The intruder—probably Ronnie Drayton—could have planted the tracker before struggling with his estranged wife. Drops of blood that matched her husband's type were found on the floor and a heavy lamp with the same blood on it. Evidently, Isabelle clobbered him and escaped with Maisy and the diaper bag that contained the tracker."

"Makes sense. When Izzy showed up on my doorstep, she was sporting a bruise on her cheek and one on her forehead and walking with a limp."

"Ronnie must have come to and called in Seton to follow up. Since our people spotted the hired killer near Isabelle's apartment, we assumed he had found evidence there as to her destination. Now it makes more sense that he followed the transmission from the tracking device to your house."

Lara hugged herself against an inner chill. "The tracking device is also a better explanation as to how those thugs picked up our trail and found us at the convenience store."

"It is that."

"But why kidnap your computer technician if they had a tracker on us?"

Ethan's shoulders rippled. "They weren't getting results with the tracker alone. We were holding them off successfully. Finding out where we were going before we got there gave them the opportunity to get ahead of us."

"Thankfully, we survived that attempt, also. I hope your technician recovers. I'll be praying for him. What a horrible experience for him and his family."

"Yes, he has a wife and two young children. I'll join you in your prayers."

Maisy started whimpering and sucking her fist.

Lara caressed the reddish fluff on top of the child's head. "You've been so patient with this bedlam in your life, especially all this time spent in your child seat. I can't help that, but I *can* feed you."

She rummaged in the diaper bag and came up with the can of powdered formula and an empty bottle. "Oh no! I forgot to fill the bottle with purified water," she told Ethan. "Could we pull over somewhere for just a flash so I can get a water jug from the groceries in the truck bed?"

"I'd like to put on a few more miles first."

"Okay, but we're going to do it to the tune of some healthy crying." She looked down at Maisy, who was beginning to fuss in earnest. "I'm sorry, sweet girl. We'll get you fed as soon as we can. But staying out of the hands of criminals is the priority." She turned toward Ethan. "Where are we headed now?"

"Rock Springs is the nearest city of any size. We should be able to find an obscure motel there. I apologize, though. The accommodations won't be as nice as Rogan and Trina's place."

"Like I told Maisy, keeping away from the Draytons and their hirelings is the priority."

Ethan suddenly let out a growl. "Tighten your seat belt. We've got company."

"Company?" Lara whipped her head around to look behind them. A dark blue sedan was rapidly catching up with them. Heat sparked through her chest. "Maybe they're just people driving down the same road we are, and they're in a bigger hurry."

"I hope you're right."

"But you don't think so.

"Call it a hunch, or maybe it's the lack of a front license plate."

"I didn't notice that." Lara gulped. "How

did they find us already? We disabled the tracker."

"We did, but I imagine they were already on the way, and when we weren't where they lost the signal, they kept on coming down the road. I was hoping we'd get far enough away that they wouldn't be able to pick up our trail. Wyoming is beautiful for wide-open spaces, but it's a little sparse on getaway routes, so here we are."

"What are we going to do?" Her heart was pounding in her throat.

The enemy car drew near enough for her to make out silhouettes of male figures in the front seat. Armed to the teeth, no doubt.

"Let them catch up to us," he said, tone casual.

She turned and glared at Ethan. "What kind of a terrible idea is that?"

Ethan sent a grim smile over his shoulder toward her. His gambit better work, because it was the only thing he could come up with. Whether he was convinced the plan could succeed or not, he needed to help Lara believe it.

"This truck is built for power, not speed," he said. "We can't outrun them. They may have superior numbers, and they may even wave their guns around a bit, but they're going to be hesitant to shoot into the cab because of the baby's presence. However, *we* have the advantage in vehicular muscle."

"They won't be able to shoot us or shove us off the road. So far, so good. How does that get them off our trail before they call in all kinds of reinforcements?"

"It's going to be up to me to find the right opportunity to force *them* off the road or to wreck their car so badly they can't follow us."

"Sounds dangerous."

"Far less than letting them pull us over."

"Agreed, but whatever you're going to do, you should do it quickly. They're gaining on us."

"I see that." Ethan was keeping an eye on the status in the side and rearview mirrors as the enemy vehicle loomed ever nearer. "Are you two buckled in extra tight back there?"

"We are."

The passenger-side window of the pursuing car rolled down, and a man leaned out, gripping a gun. All doubt as to the identities of the people in the vehicle disappeared.

A shot rang out.

"I thought you said they wouldn't fire at us," Lara cried out.

"They're aiming for a tire in order to force us to stop. I can't let them hit one. Hang on."

He slammed on the brakes. In the next split second, the pursuit car rammed the truck's rear end. The jolt carried up Ethan's spine and rattled his brain but not enough to keep him from letting up on the brake and pressing the gas to shoot away from the enemy vehicle. With a throaty growl, the truck surged ahead.

"Everyone okay back there?"

He had to raise his voice because Maisy's crying had ramped up a notch. Now the poor kid was hungry *and* scared, but a least she wasn't in the clutches of ruthless killers.

"We're fine, Ethan. That car may have a crumpled front end, but it's still coming."

Ethan's heart dropped into his toes. These guys didn't know when to quit. Plan B, then. Good thing traffic was nonexistent at the moment. As the car crept toward them and swung out to pull up beside them, Ethan jerked the wheel and cut them off. Tires screeched and metal ground against metal. The car backed off.

"You did more damage," Lara said, "but they're still coming. And that shooter is start-

ing to stick his head out the window again."
Her voice hitched.

"I know, hang on."

Ethan rammed the brakes, and the pursuing
car must have done the same, because there
was no collision. However, the shooter jerked
and fell back inside the car.

"Temporary reprieve," Lara announced.
Her tone had gone high and tight.

Heat flared deep in Ethan's chest. What
right did twisted people like this have to in-
flict such threat and terror on decent folks
who wanted only to do the right thing? He
hit the brakes again and was rewarded by a
metallic crunch.

"How are we doing?" he asked his adult
passenger.

"That car must have nine lives. Still coming, though I think I see a hint of steam coming from under the buckled hood."

"Progress, then."

"Yes, but what if that shooter tries again
and succeeds?"

Plan C, then. Ethan pulled his service
weapon from its holster.

"Stop!" Lara snapped. "There's no way
you're going to be able to safely control this

vehicle *and* take potshots at our pursuers at the same time. Give me the gun."

"You know how to shoot?"

"I hike wilderness trails as part of my living. Often alone. What do you think? I'm going to pop *their* tire."

Without another word, Ethan handed her his pistol, but his gut went tense as a bowstring. What if she missed her shot, and the gunman in the car did not?

"Thank you," she said. "Now let them get a little closer."

"If you say so."

"I do."

Taut silence fell over the vehicle. Even Maisy's crying had cut back to a few whimpers. Was he making a huge mistake yielding the shot to Lara? What choice did he have? She was right. He couldn't safely operate the truck and shoot at the bad guys at the same time. He had to trust God and trust Lara.

The pursuit car crept up on them once more, the driver displaying extra caution in the gradual approach.

"That's it!" Lara's voice was a hissed whisper as her window swooshed down.

"Be careful."

Ethan's words of caution were drowned out

by an angry feminine growl. "I'll teach you to go around slinging bullets at a vehicle with a baby on board."

Gritting his teeth and praying, Ethan kept an eye on the rear-and side-view mirrors. Lara poked her torso out the window, aiming even as the shooter in the car leaned out, pistol brandished.

A shot sounded.

Who'd fired? Lara or the thug in the car?

EIGHT

Lara's muscles went weak as a half-drowned kitten's, and she melted against her door. She'd hit the enemy's tire with the first shot. Her jaw dropped and her heart lifted as the pursuit car fishtailed all over the road. Finally, the vehicle plowed into a ditch and smacked up against a tree. The threat of Draytons' thugs faded in the rear window.

"That was some shooting."

Ethan's appreciative words roused Lara from her slump.

"I surprised myself," she answered a bit breathlessly.

"At first, when you went limp, I was afraid you were hit."

"Sorry to scare you. I was just so astonished and grateful to have hit what I aimed at. I do well at the gun range, but I've never had to shoot at a moving target. Not even an animal in the woods, much less a vehicle with people inside it."

"You continue to amaze me. Not many people ever have to do something like that, so now you've had a unique experience you could have done without."

Lara hauled in a deep cleansing breath. "You can say that again."

"I'll refrain." His brief chuckle held a wry flavor. "We need to get off this road and head somewhere they'll never guess. Any ideas?"

Lara blinked at Ethan. This law enforcement professional was humble and secure enough to ask *her* for ideas? If she'd needed any further proof that Ethan Ridgeway didn't share any of her ex-fiancé's control issues, here it was. But that didn't mean she could regard this man as an eligible bachelor, despite her reluctant attraction to him. Their relationship was protector to protectee, period.

"We-e-ell," she drawled as her thoughts sought to organize themselves. "There are lots of side roads. Most of them are gravel, though many have magnificent views at their dead ends. I know that from some of my explorations."

"No side roads, then. I'm seeing signs for

Highway 189. You seem to know the area. Where should we go?"

"Yes, 189 is good. Let's do it."

"That'll take us down to the Big Piney area."

"Then if we swing west on Highway 350, we'll come to Bridger-Teton National Forest. I know a forest ranger named Jake there who will gladly help us hide out in a ranger cabin deep in the woods. You up for roughing it?"

"Can't get much rougher than it's been." Ethan shook his head as he took the turn onto Highway 189. "Your friend, is he a romantic interest? Not trying to be nosy. Just trying to gauge how strongly he's going to react to us showing up with you in danger."

"Romantic? Not at all." Lara laughed. "We met when I did a vlog about the national forest last year. He was very helpful and very much in love with his girlfriend."

"That's good then."

Did she detect a note of relief in Ethan's tone? What was that about? Was he glad that Jake and she weren't a couple, or was she reading something personal into Ethan's reaction that was intended to be purely professional? They guy was so hard to read sometimes when he waffled between warm friendliness to all stiff and businesslike from one moment to the next.

Shaking her head, Lara settled into her seat and gave her attention to Maisy. The little girl was screwing up her face again for a big wail.

"I know, I know, little one," she told the child. "Soon now."

"Here's a wayside rest," Ethan said. "I'll pull over but just long enough for you to grab water for the baby."

"Consider it done."

Soon they were on the road again, and Maisy was happily feasting on her formula.

"Should be a quiet trip now." She smiled at the little girl.

"I hope so. I could use some peace and quiet."

Lara added a silent *Amen.* Heaviness settled over her body and mind. As soon as Maisy finished her bottle and drifted toward sleep, Lara laid her head back against her seat. She wouldn't close her eyes, of course. Slumber beckoned, but she'd have to resist until they landed in their safe place in the forest.

"Lara!" Something brushed her arm.

Ethan's urgent tone and gentle touch jerked Lara awake. She sat up with a start. She'd let herself fall asleep. Time had passed and dusk had closed in around them. They were stopped in a wooded area. Nearby stood a low-slung log building illuminated by a single bulb over the small stoop. The truck engine was idling, but Ethan had got out, opened her door and was gazing at her with furrowed brow.

"I'm so sorry I nodded off," she said.

He grinned. "I'm not. You needed the rest. It's been a big day."

"I've never experienced one like it."

"And I hope you never do again, but we're not out of the woods yet—pun intended."

Lara dredged up a smile. "Are we at the entrance to the forest?"

"We are, but it doesn't look like anyone is in the office." He gestured toward the small log building.

"No worries. My friend lives only a hundred yards or so up the road."

"On the forest grounds?"

"Yes, he's the primary caretaker."

"Onward, then." He got in and put the vehicle in motion.

They glided slowly up an unpaved road skirted by trees. Shortly, the lights of a modest-sized home appeared ahead.

"Here we are," Lara said. "Go ahead and

park. I'll get out and talk to Jake. You'd better stay here with Maisy. She's just waking up from a nap." The little girl was stirring and whisking a hand against her face in the infant approximation of rubbing her eyes.

"Hmm." Ethan turned his head and met her gaze. "I'm not happy about you going in alone. We haven't exactly done well with our safe havens today."

"Me going in alone probably isn't going to be necessary," she said, motioning toward a bulky figure exiting the house and stepping down the front walk toward them. "We've been spotted. That's Jake."

Lara rolled down her window. "Hey, Jake. It's me, Lara Werth."

"Lara?" The big man strolled up to the window and peered inside. "What are you doing here at this hour? And with a baby in tow?"

"Long story. But meet Deputy Marshal Ethan Ridgeway behind the wheel there."

Ethan obligingly showed his badge.

"Little Maisy and I are in some version of witness protection," she went on, "until some very bad people can be apprehended and put behind bars. We're looking for a safe place to go to ground for a while."

Jake let out a low whistle. "For real?"

"I wish I could say it wasn't."

"Wow. That's tough. Come on in. I've got a spare bedroom and a comfy couch."

"That's very generous of you," Ethan put in. "But it's probably not a good idea if we stay at your place. We're dangerous guests at the moment."

Jake's brow puckered. "What can I do for you, then?"

"We're hoping we can hide out in one of the ranger cabins for a few days," Lara said.

Jake pursed his lips, then let out a long breath. "I think that could be arranged. Let me go inside and get a key."

"Do you mind if I use your cell phone before we take off?" Ethan asked. "I need to call my headquarters for an update, and I don't dare put the battery back in my cell, because the bad guys may have the number and be able to locate us."

"Cloak-and-dagger, for sure." Jake dug in his pants pocket. "Here you go." He passed the phone to Lara, who handed it to Ethan. "Be back in a sec."

Lara sat forward as Ethan put the call through. What would be the news about her mother? Logic told her she had nothing to feel guilty for regarding her mother's injury and endangerment, but someone had forgotten to give her heart the memo. None of this would be happening if Lara hadn't opened her door to Izzy and Maisy. Yet Mom would be the first person to tell her she'd done the only right thing by taking them in, and Lara would do it again in a heartbeat anyway. So, here they were, precariously surviving, and they had to see this thing through.

"This is Terry," Ethan's partner answered the phone.

Lara smiled her gratitude at Ethan for putting the call on speaker.

"Ethan here with Lara listening in."

"I hoped it was you when I didn't recognize the number. But I'm impressed how you manage to come up with all these different phones to call me from."

"Borrowing one right now," Ethan answered and then filled in his partner on the discovery of the GPS device and their subsequent flight from his friends' home. "The bad guys caught up with us on the road, but Lara shot out one of their tires and we left them in a ditch."

Terry barked a laugh. "You go, Annie Oakley!"

Lara's face heated. "I got angry. Must have improved my aim."

"Whatever it was," Ethan put in, "it saved the day, and we're off-grid and out of sight now. Don't ask where."

"What's the news on my mother?" Lara asked.

"Awake and improved enough that she's demanding updates on you every two seconds and mighty mad that we don't tell her much except you're alive."

A tiny laugh escaped Lara's lips. "Sounds like Mom. Please give her my love and don't tell her anything else."

"Count on it," Terry answered.

"Progress report on locating the Draytons?" Ethan asked.

"No sign of them, including Isabelle. It's like they've melted into the landscape."

Lara's heart fell. When were they going to catch a break?

Ethan hauled the last of the groceries into the small cabin Jake had loaned them. They'd driven several miles into the forest to get to the cozy single-room dwelling, but it had a loft for Lara and the baby to sleep in and he could take the more-than-adequate long leather couch. From her perch on said couch, playing with a chortling Maisy, Lara sent him a smile as he walked past her into the kitchen area.

"Hungry?" he asked.

"Famished."

"It's late for any complicated cooking, but how about I heat up that canned beef stew?" He began stowing goods in the cupboards.

"I might be tempted to eat shoe leather if I have to wait much longer, so bring it on." She chuckled.

The mellow sound warmed Ethan's heart. It was good to hear her relaxed. Hopefully, she could get a good night's sleep, though with Maisy having recently awakened from a nap, how soon any of them would be able to turn in for the night depended on when the baby was ready to go down. He opened the foam cooler that contained milk and a few perishables on ice—items they'd obtained at the convenience store this afternoon—and put the food away in the refrigerator. Then he heated up the stew.

They gobbled down their supper, keeping their conversation light. Then they played with Maisy until she started to get fussy. Lara changed her while Ethan mixed formula. The little girl fell asleep as she neared the bottom of her bottle. Lara looked up from the infant and smiled at him. Ethan's heart did a somersault. This woman was too sweet and brave and beautiful for his peace of mind.

"I think she's down for the night," she whispered to him.

"There was a large clothes basket up in the loft," he whispered back. "I lined it with blankets for Maisy's bed."

"Thank you," she mouthed at him and rose. "Good night."

Ethan's gaze followed her lithe figure up the stairs. She disappeared into the loft, and he released the breath he hadn't known he was holding.

This whole misadventure was giving him firsthand experience in how much caring for an infant affected every aspect of life. Child rearing was a huge responsibility, but strangely, he liked it…and being around Lara. This domesticity was far too appealing.

Head in the game, he told himself. He needed to put his mind to devising some way to draw the Draytons out without endangering Lara or Maisy. A tall order.

Ethan prowled to one of the windows, parted the curtain and peered outside. Moonlight spread a hazy glow across the clearing where the cabin sat. Their pickup, with its somewhat damaged rear end, was parked near to the door in case they had to make a quick getaway. Outside, an owl hooted and crickets chirped. The scene was idyllic and peaceful. No sign of enemy intrusion.

The respite was more than welcome, but that didn't mean Ethan could afford to sleep tonight. He needed to stand watch. Maybe tomorrow he'd grab a nap while Lara was awake. After that, once they were reasonably certain they'd disappeared from enemy radar, he'd risk sleeping at night.

Time passed slowly, and thankfully, it stayed quiet. Ethan busied himself with small chores like a little food prep for tomorrow and cleaning his gun. When the new day dawned, he would go back to Jake's place and see if the ranger had a rifle or shotgun they could borrow. He hadn't thought of it when they first arrived, but a single pistol wasn't much of a defensive weapon against the sort of firepower the Draytons could bring. And now that he knew how well Lara could shoot, more than one weapon made extra sense.

At around one, a sharp cry from above raised the hairs on the back of Ethan's neck.

A series of moans followed, then a hoarse, "No! No!"

Ethan snatched his pistol and rushed up the stairs. Had someone managed to climb in through the small window in the loft? He was sure he'd locked it, and he certainly hadn't heard any glass break.

He arrived at Lara's side to find her thrashing in the bed, twisting her covers, but she was alone and clearly still asleep. She tossed her head on the pillow, but her eyes were pinched closed in the grip of a nightmare. He needed to be cautious and gentle when awakening her, or she might literally almost hit the ceiling from being startled.

He placed a firm hand on one of her shoulders. Tension radiated up his arm from her taut muscles.

"Lara." He spoke in a soft but urgent tone and shook her slightly. "Wake up."

She jerked and went rigid, then her eyes popped open. Her glassy gaze darted around, as if searching for the source of danger. A long exhale suddenly left her lips, and her body relaxed as her attention focused on him.

"I'm sorry," she whispered and sat up, clutching the blanket under her chin. "Bad dream."

"Understandable."

Maisy whimpered and stirred in her basket.

Lara put her fingers to her lips. "I'm not going back to sleep anytime soon." Her voice was barely audible. "I'll join you downstairs in a minute."

Ethan nodded and returned to the living room. His limbs had that wet-noodle feel in the wake of a surge of adrenaline. Silently, he thanked God that the danger, for once, had not been real.

Soon, Lara arrived downstairs. She'd donned jeans and a T-shirt, but her feet were bare. Her dainty toes sported an attractive shade of turquoise nail polish.

"Feeling better now?" Ethan asked.

Lara put a hand to her chest. "Much. My heart doesn't feel like it's about to leap out of my chest."

Ethan held up a small package in each hand. "The water is already hot on the stove, and I can offer you tea or cocoa. I'm guessing the former, because that's what you chose at Amy's house."

"Where did you get the tea and cocoa? We didn't pick any up at the convenience store."

"It was here in the cupboard."

"Nice! And you're right. Tea, definitely."

Ethan looked at the label. "Chamomile. Might help you relax again and go back to sleep."

"I hope so." She yawned as she sat down on the sofa. "Have you slept at all?"

"Keeping watch."

"Thank you, but I'm sorry you're not getting any rest."

"No worries. I'm enjoying the lack of excitement."

"Until my nightmare antics." She let out a brief laugh.

He handed Lara a steaming mug with a tea bag steeping inside. Then, wrapping his fingers around his mug of cocoa, he settled into a wooden rocking chair near the unlit fireplace. As cozy as a fire might be, the summer weather was too warm to make additional heat comfortable.

"Let's hunker down here for a few days and get our bearings," he told Lara. "But if my people don't make progress soon locating and arresting Vinnie and Ronnie Drayton, we may have to consider becoming more proactive."

She froze with her mug halfway to her lips. "What did you have in mind?" Her stare lasered into him.

"Some ideas have been rolling around in my brain, but I haven't arrived at a plan I totally like. They all—"

"Carry risk," she finished for him, frowning. "I knew we'd eventually be used as bait."

Ethan's heart squeezed in on itself. If only he could deny the charge, but there was no play-it-safe option that he could see. Not if they wanted this for-real nightmare to be over sometime within the foreseeable future.

NINE

"Level with me about the possibilities," Lara said, setting her mug on the side table. Her stomach was rolling too badly to tolerate anything. What was she being maneuvered into? She needed to lay down some ground rules. "I'm telling you up front that *none* of these plans will involve Maisy."

"Goes without saying," Ethan answered and took a deep breath as if he would continue speaking.

She held up a forestalling hand. "I understand that I'm going to have to feature in these ploys to draw out the Draytons, so don't try to soft-pedal anything."

The edges of his lips quirked slightly upward, but his gaze was somber. "You've caught me trying to hold back once too often, so I won't try it again. But please understand that whatever *we* decide on, you will be surrounded and protected on all sides by well-trained members of the marshals service."

"I have no doubt about that, but I've also experienced the determination, persistence and sheer numbers of our enemies."

"It's good that you know firsthand what we're up against. Any plan needs to include two essential factors—minimizing the numbers arrayed against us and drawing out the Draytons themselves, not merely their hired guns."

"What have you come up with so far?" Lara reclaimed her tea, blew on it and ventured a sip.

His use of the term *we* assured her that any plan would include her input and require her approval. She needed to stop indulging this knee-jerk reaction against manipulation and control born of her experience with Matt. It was time for her to trust Ethan.

If only she could…completely. Despite his assurance that he'd stop holding back, he was still concealing something pivotal. His conflicted reactions to her, one minute formal and the next familiar, told her that much. It could be something from his own past, or the issue could be work related. Whatever it was, he needed to deal with it so they could move forward in sync. Lives were at stake.

"Before we put our heads together to come up with a plan, I need to ask what it is that makes you so uncomfortable around me at times."

He blinked at her, face blank. "Excuse me, what are you talking about?"

"Puh-lease. You keep bouncing back and forth between Mr. Friendly and Mr. Arm's Length. I never know exactly who I'm dealing with—the guy who cares about me as a person or the guy who regards me as an assignment."

Ethan's face washed white and then went red as a stoplight. Lara braced herself for a snarl and a scold at being questioned and confronted. Then she ordered herself to relax. This man was not Matt. He could surprise her and respond reasonably.

"It's not you. It's me!" he burst out, then he spluttered and threw his hands up. "Sorry, that sounded really dumb. But I'm serious. It's my problem. I had a—a bad experience a while back. Probably about the time you were having your own bad experience with that jerk of a fiancé."

At his choice of words about Matt, Lara

couldn't contain a laugh. "That's exactly what my mother calls him."

Ethan shifted in his seat and offered a vague grin that was almost a grimace, like he couldn't decide whether to be amused at the coincidence or terrified about the conversation they were having. Probably a combination of both.

Lara leaned toward him. "It's okay. You don't have to give me details about what happened. And I'm not saying we need to be best buds. I understand that you're operating in a professional capacity, and I definitely want you to be at the top of your game, but I do want you to be yourself around me. That way I can relax around *you*."

Ethan released a long gush of air. "Fair enough. I should have guessed you would pick up on the mixed messages I didn't mean to be sending. You challenge me, Lara. You really do."

"Because I question you?"

"Not at all." His gaze met hers. "Neither your independence nor your caution bothers me."

"Then what is it?"

He rose. "I'll refresh your tea and then fill you in."

"Am I right to deduce the story might be a bit long?"

"Not necessarily, but I think I'm going to need refreshment to tell it."

The sad smile he sent her way wrung Lara's heart. What could have happened to daunt this brave and determined man?

Less than a minute later, Ethan took a seat beside Lara on the couch. He leaned forward, elbows on knees, and gripping his mug in both hands. Lara sat back, sipping her tea. She could wait as long as it took for him to get his thoughts together. This was not a moment to rush.

"I was a newbie in the marshals service," he began at last, "stationed in Maryland, and we caught a case where we had to protect a whole multigenerational family until a murder trial of an extremely bad guy could take place. We had an older man, his daughter, his son-in-law and his toddler grandson to look after. It was the son-in-law who was going to testify, but it was the grandpa who sucked me in."

"Sucked you in? That's a strange phrase to use."

He glanced over his shoulder at her, gaze shadowed. "It's accurate."

"Since this is work related, is it okay for you to be telling me this?"

He shrugged. "The case is a matter of public record now, so I don't see why not."

"Okay. Go ahead." She leaned forward, elbows on knees, mirroring his posture in a suggestion of empathy.

"Joseph—that was his name—reminded me so much of my own grandfather it was eerie. My granddad had passed away a few years earlier, and I missed him a lot. This guy had similar looks and mannerisms, some of the same speech patterns, and they even laughed the same way. It was instinctive for me to trust him. What I didn't realize until it was almost too late is that this man and my grandfather didn't share the same character."

"Am I sensing a betrayal theme here?"

"Sharp, as usual." He turned his head her way and smiled.

Their gazes locked, his face inches from hers. Lara's heart went pitter-patter like a schoolgirl with a new crush. The man simply took her breath away, especially in this moment of open vulnerability. If it didn't sound sappy, she'd say she could see into his soul and it was beautiful.

Ethan's gaze drifted toward her mouth.

Lara held her breath, unable—no, unwilling—to pull back.

Then he looked away and sat up, breaking the connection. He was doing that warm-cool thing again, even as he was attempting to explain to her why. She drew in a deep breath. His withdrawal was for the best. This was no time or place for romance. In fact, kissing her would probably be a breach of professional ethics for him.

Lara cleared her throat and took a sip of her tea. The warm fluid soothed her tight throat. Of course, she was relieved the intimate moment had passed. If only she could make herself believe she wouldn't give her right arm to experience that kiss. The Draytons might be the biggest threat to her life, but the man next to her was becoming the biggest threat to her heart.

Ethan gulped down a big breath of air. That was a close call. He'd come within a millisecond of kissing the woman he was supposed to be protecting. Next to him, Lara sat stiffly sipping her tea and not sparing him a glance. Had she, too, felt the urge to join their lips together? If so, did he dare hope she was disappointed the kiss hadn't happened? Or was she offended that he had again sent her that conflicted on-again, off-again message?

Clearly, he'd have to level with her 100 percent. He needed her to trust him protect her the way she deserved to be protected. Lara was a gem in every way, and he couldn't—wouldn't—allow the Draytons to deprive the world of her or take possession of little Maisy.

Ethan rose and went to the rocking chair. "I'm sorry about that. Usually, I'm able to maintain complete professional distance, but honestly, with you, I'm struggling. Not because I *don't* like you but because I *do*. Too much."

Color washed up Lara's neck and onto her cheeks. "Really?" The word squeaked out her mouth.

"But that's not okay. Not right now. This feeling reminds me of the time I let my guard down with someone under my care. Innocent people were nearly killed because I allowed the relationship to become so personal that my professional judgment was impaired."

Her eyes narrowed and she canted her head at him. "I see. Well, sort of, since you haven't finished your story, but I totally agree that now is a terrible time to allow feelings to develop and relationships to become personal. I'm struggling with that myself."

"Really?" It was his turn for a word to pop out in a higher-than-normal tone of voice.

His heart did a little jig. She was attracted to him? That was great. No, that was terrible. Ethan scrubbed a hand over his face.

"I guess I'd better finish telling you what happened. Then maybe you'll understand the risks of clouded judgment in our sort of situation better."

"Go ahead, please." She set her mug on the side table and fixed her gaze on him.

"My partner at the time and I were sequestered with this family for several weeks. The toddler was adorable but active and a challenge. The kid didn't seem to take to me, hence my earlier comment about questioning my compatibility with children. The boy's mother was jittery and scared, which may have contributed to her child's wild behavior. The father was determined to do the right thing by testifying and putting this dangerous man behind bars, but I could tell he was scared, too."

"Understandable." Lara nodded at him.

"Right. But Grandpa seemed the cool, calm and reasonable hand at the helm of the family unit, and by the end of three weeks, I respected and trusted him completely."

"But?"

"Yes, big *but* in there. What I didn't know was that he was the most frightened of them all but hid it behind a jolly mask. I had started equating him with *my* grandfather, who was a true stalwart, steady as a rock. But in reality, this guy was all bravado and no foundation. He had no faith or trust in me—or more accurately, in the marshals service."

Lara frowned. "He didn't believe you'd be able to protect him and his family?"

"Correct. Since there was no reason to believe our location was compromised, we were allowed to go outdoors for some recreation. The house we were in was on a secluded beach, so we would take the tot down to the water's edge to build sandcastles and run off some energy.

"But one day, Grandpa said he was too tired and wanted to take a nap while we were at the beach. I totally understood—or thought I did—that the old guy just wanted some peace and quiet and alone time. I didn't blame him a bit. I was gone about ten minutes helping the little family take all the equipment down to the beach—chairs, umbrellas, toys and what-not. By the time I got back to the house to keep watch, the damage had been done. I just didn't know it yet."

Wide-eyed, Lara leaned forward. "What did he do?"

"He got on my laptop and made an internet call to one of the bad guy's pals, betraying our location on the condition that he, his daughter and his grandson were spared."

Lara gasped and covered her mouth with a hand. "That's awful. Let me guess. A short time later, you were ambushed at that beach house by hired thugs, much like the ones we've been fighting off."

"You got it. A small army of them, as it turns out."

"Was anyone hurt?"

"Only minor injuries on our side, thankfully."

"You and your partner held off an army?"

"Briefly. A short time before the attack came, I noticed someone had been on the laptop recently, and I knew it wasn't me or my partner. There was only one person who'd been in the house alone for any length of time. I confronted Grandpa, and he caved pretty quickly. Confessed what he'd done out of sheer panic at the prospect of what the bad guy *might* arrange to have happen to his family if his son-in-law testified. I called the situation in, and as we were preparing to vacate the house, the attackers arrived. My partner and I held down the fort under fire for hair-raising minutes and then the cavalry arrived from multiple law enforcement agencies."

Lara was shaking her head repeatedly. "That's—that's amazing! Did the son-in-law ever testify?"

"He did, but his relationship with his father-in-law was shattered by the man's betrayal. And, as you can imagine, it devastated the man's daughter that he was willing to sacrifice her husband's life. I didn't stay in touch, so I don't know how the family fared in the long run, but the stress was huge, so—" He ended the thought with a wordless shrug.

"I don't see any reason to blame you for the incident." Her words were spoken hotly, as if she were ready to step up and defend him.

He held up a quieting hand and lowered his head, staring at his shoes. "The marshals service investigated the incident thoroughly, and my partner and I were commended. They determined there had been no violation of procedure. After all, it's *not* reasonable to suspect a person you're protecting with your life would reach out to the enemy. But I've always blamed myself for getting too comfortable with the man and allowing him the opportunity."

Lara sniffed as she stood up and took his empty mug from him. "To me, it sounds like you treated him with common courtesy. No more nor less than anyone should receive under your supervision. Do you want my honest opinion?"

"Sounds like I'm going to get it." He gazed up at her, and something thawed inside him at the fierce earnestness of her expression. The woman was the essence of sincerity and transparency.

"I don't think you feel guilty on a procedural level." She wagged a finger at him. "You didn't do anything wrong and your head knows that. I think you're blaming yourself for being fooled by someone who turned out to be untrustworthy. Like it's a sign of weakness. News flash! You're human. We all place trust where we shouldn't from time to time."

Ethan rose with a frown "In my position, I can't afford those kinds of mistakes. People's lives are on the line."

She stuck out her chin, undaunted. "Too bad. You're *going* to make mistakes whether you can afford to or not. It's how quickly you recover from those mistakes and take the next right action that counts. Trying to be the ice man and shutting out personal feelings is *not* the answer."

Ethan spluttered a laugh. "Are you sure you didn't major in philosophy in college?"

"Psychology, actually. Photography was my hobby until it became my profession."

"Interesting. Well, right now I believe my next right action is to urge you to go back to bed and get some more rest. Morning's coming quickly."

She glanced at her watch. "Three a.m. That means I should have time for three more hours of shut-eye before the pint-size princess wakes up demanding her breakfast."

"You know Maisy's schedule already?"

"It's on her mother's list for me, and the timing proved true yesterday morning. Hopefully, our wild day didn't disrupt that schedule. I've heard it's good for babies to have a routine."

"Off to bed, then. Thank you for hearing me out."

"Thank you for telling me. I know it was difficult." She sent him a soft smile as she headed away.

Ethan's heart lightened as she retreated up the stairs. Is that all he'd really needed? To unburden himself to someone who not only understood but was willing to call him out on his attitude? Not that he was sure she was right. He'd have to give some thought to what she'd said. Later. When this was over.

He'd give his people more time to come up with leads, but it could well come down to the last-ditch ploy of using Lara for bait. He still needed to figure out how to reel in the Draytons without her getting hurt or Maisy coming anywhere near her ruthless relatives.

The following days passed uneventfully and stretched into a week. They fell into a cycle of sleeping, playing with Maisy, hiking outdoors with lots of picture taking, cooking and eating together. Lara said routine was good for the baby, and apparently routine was good for the adults, as well. He and Lara were markedly more relaxed around each other but still both vigilant.

She continued to be the sort of protectee who asked lots of pertinent questions. In fact, they spent a little while each day discussing options for drawing the Draytons into the open. The conversation always ended with him recommending they give his people a little space to find the crooks another way. Any scenario that involved her as bait felt too risky.

Ethan found Lara as attractive as ever, but they seemed to have reached a tacit agreement that exploring personal feelings was off the table. For now, at least. Caring for the baby was a handy buffer between them.

Lara's forest ranger friend, Jake, brought them a burner phone, and Ethan used it morning and evening to check in with Terry. Ethan had given him the serial number of the tracker they'd discovered in the baby toy in hopes of it leading to the purchaser. No results on that yet, but to Lara's relief, they found out that her mother was recovering nicely from the injury she'd received during the kidnapping attempt and had been taken to a new safe house that hadn't been on record when the US Marshals Service computer system had been hacked. Also, Alex Bingham, that kidnapped computer tech, had awakened from his coma and was expected to recover completely, though the ketamine had ensured he didn't remember much about his ordeal.

Other than those bits of good news, there were no fresh leads on finding the Draytons. Hearing daily that there was a lack of development was the only unwelcome aspect of their routine.

Jake had also brought them a shotgun, which Ethan kept loaded and ready for trouble.

A week to the day after they'd arrived at their national forest haven, Jake arrived on their front porch to deliver the groceries and infant supplies they'd asked him to pick up. Ethan took one look at the tension lines around Jake's mouth and moved outside, closing the door after him. Lara was inside, humming to Maisy as she fed the child a bottle.

"What's going on?" he asked Jake in a low tone.

"I don't know how much time you'll have to make yourselves scarce, but I think your enemies might suspect you're holed up in this forest."

TEN

Lara opened the door and stepped onto the porch, cradling the baby in her arms. "Don't be trying to hide anything from me," she told the two men, glaring from one to the other.

"How did you know?" Ethan scratched his head.

"When Jake shows up, he marches right in." She motioned toward her forest ranger friend, then jerked her chin at Ethan. "*You* don't go outside and close the door."

He raised his hands in a surrender gesture. If this were a time for levity, she'd laugh at the red on his face.

"Spill!" she ordered Jake, who also had a slightly pink face. "What happened?

He raised the bags he carried in his hands. "I got this stuff at the grocery store in Big Piney. As I was checking out, I noticed a couple of burly hard cases standing around watching people. An old friend who works there was checking my groceries and started to make conversation. 'You got company with a baby?' he says. Those hard cases perked right up."

"Did they approach you?" Ethan relieved Jake of the bag holding the baby supplies.

"They started to trail me as I headed for my truck in the parking lot, but just then, a cop car pulled in. The officers got out and started asking these guys questions. Evidently, the presence of strangers lurking around like scary vagrants had bothered other folks, and someone had called the police to check them out."

Lara popped the empty bottle out of Maisy's mouth, put the child on her shoulder and began to pat her back. "So you got away without being followed?"

"Yeah." Jake frowned. "But I'm not fooling myself that they won't come looking for me as soon as they can, expecting to find you three. And they'll know where to hunt me up. They saw me in my uniform, and this is the only national forest in the vicinity. I'm sorry, but those guys and some of their pals might even now be preparing to storm the forest."

Lara's heart dipped into her toes. This refuge in the forest had seemed idyllic, a calm cocoon of protection for their little pseudo-family to rest in. Something about it had felt like time had stopped for them while the out-side world went on spinning. Now the respite was at an abrupt end, and the threat was clos-ing in again.

Ethan jerked a decisive nod. "Our presence in the forest is known—or at least suspected. Drayton's people will be along anytime to search every campground and cabin for us. We need to get out of here ASAP."

"Won't take me more than a few minutes to repack my go bag," she said, heading into the cabin with Maisy, who had done her burp-ing and was now cooing and blowing bubbles. The men followed her inside.

"I'll throw together Maisy's things," Jake offered.

"Do it," Ethan said. "I need to call Terry about our situation and ask him to send in whatever law enforcement is available. Then we have to get going." He turned toward Jake. "Buddy, you need to warn your fellow rangers and other personnel throughout the forest and tell them not to engage these guys. None of you are trained to handle the kind of trouble hired guns can dish out."

"Don't worry. I'm out ahead on that." He winked at them. "On my way here, I got on the radio and instructed my people to give the runaround to any strangers asking questions about a couple with a baby staying in the forest. Tell them, 'Oh, yeah, I saw them here' or 'Oh, yeah, I saw them there.' Should buy us a little time to get away."

"Us?" Lara stared at her friend.

"Jake's going to have to hang with us," Ethan said, "until we shake our pursuers and can disappear again. If Drayton's goons spot him, they'll do more than ask semipolite questions, because he's the guy who was seen buying our supplies."

Tears stung the backs of Lara's eyes. "I'm sorry I got you caught up in this mess."

Jake shook his head at her. "Don't be. I'm honored you came to me."

"We're going to get through this." Ethan's tone commanded confidence.

Lara met his rock-steady gaze, and her fluttering pulse settled into a more natural rhythm. If anyone could get them to safety, it would be this man. She laid Maisy on a blanket near the hearth and left the child kicking her feet and trying to grab her toes while she went to the loft to pack. Ten minutes later, she arrived back downstairs, a strap of her go bag over one shoulder and carrying a few of Maisy's things to stuff into the child's diaper tote. Ethan and Jake already had everything else put together and were carrying it out to the pickup.

"Last load," Ethan told her. "Let's go."

Jake headed for his forest service truck, and Ethan led the way to the pickup they'd arrived in. In one hand, he carried a heavy-duty backpack bulging with supplies. In the other, he held the shotgun provided by the forest ranger. Maisy was yawning as Lara snapped the baby carrier into place in the center position of the back seat. She buckled herself in next to the child.

Ethan started the vehicle and looked over his shoulder at Lara. "Jake's going to guide us along a little-used route out of the forest that doesn't appear on publicly available maps of the forest."

"Good thinking."

The national forest vehicle pulled out, leading them away from the main exit and deeper into the woods. They soon took a turnoff onto a track so narrow that pine branches rasped against the sides of the pickup. The road was deeply shadowed by tree branches, and progress was slowed by ruts in the dirt road. The bouncing aggravated the knots in Lara's stomach, but it didn't seem to faze Maisy, who'd fallen fast asleep for her morning nap.

"In about twenty minutes," Ethan said, "we should reach a paved county road that will take us into Cokeville. Since those goons we left behind in a ditch saw this truck, Terry's going to call ahead, and a car dealer there should have a vehicle ready for us to switch out for the pickup. Then the dealer's going to hide the truck until we give the all clear. Jake's going to lie low in Cokeville, but we need to head on to Interstate 80. If we can make it to district headquarters in Cheyenne, we can take refuge there. It'll be cots to sleep on and takeout to eat, because HQ isn't set up for overnight guests, but we'll make do in a pinch."

Lara snorted a laugh. "I'll take a cot and boxed lunches any day for the luxury of safety. If the Draytons discover where we are but see they can't get to us, isn't that going to drive them to desperate measures? My mom will be in more danger than ever."

"You'll have to trust the marshals service to look after her."

Lara's heart squeezed in on itself. Ethan

had shared with her a scary and dangerous incident when he and his people had been betrayed by a frightened person under their protection, nearly costing many innocent lives. Yet, she had a glimmer of understanding what had driven the old man from Ethan's story to make the fateful choice. Of course, the marshals service would do their utmost to protect her mother, Maisy and her, but the outcome was anything but guaranteed. As long as the Draytons remained at large, anything could happen, and the hunt for the criminals seemed no closer to ending than it had when this whole episode had begun.

"We're almost out of the woods," Ethan said with a slight chuckle at the obvious pun.

Lara spirits lifted. Brightness beckoned at the end of the narrow tunnel between the trees.

"Whoa!" Ethan cried out.

A sudden jerk threw Lara forward against her seat belt and brought a yip from Maisy, who startled awake. The truck abruptly halted nearly on top of Jake's bumper. Lara peered ahead through Jake's rear window. Her friend was motioning frantically for them to back up. Ethan flung his arm over the back of his seat and swiveled his head to the rear. The tires spun as the truck surged into retreat.

Pulse throbbing, Lara looked behind them. Ethan was going to have his hands full keeping them on the bumpy narrow track in fast reverse. She looked ahead of them, and her heart leaped into her throat. Beyond Jake's pickup, a massive black SUV charged toward them. They were under attack!

Ethan fought to stay on the slim road. Clearly, their enemies had gained quick access to a nonpublic map of the forest that included the service roads, and here they were, waiting at the end of the trail. Drayton's people probably had the forest surrounded.

A crash and screech of metal drew Ethan's attention forward. Jake's pickup was sideways across the track, and the oncoming enemy vehicle had collided with it. Had Jake turned his truck into a roadblock on purpose? There was no time or opportunity to investigate. Armed thugs were piling out of the SUV. Ethan swiveled his head and continued guiding their truck backward on the rutted road.

"What about Jake?" Lara cried.

Ethan's heart wrung at the tremor in her voice. If only there were some way to aid the man who had helped them, but he wasn't going to waste the opportunity Jake had given them to put distance between a crew of rabid thugs and his precious cargo.

"We can't stop," he said. "Hopefully, they won't bother him in their haste to come after us."

"We can't back up all the way to our cabin. They'll be waiting for us there, too."

Nothing wrong with Lara's deductive faculties.

"I saw a road even rougher than this one veering off to the left with a sign that said Dead End," he told her. "We'll follow it as far as we can go. Then we'll have to hike. Jake put that infant harness he bought for us to use on our walks into the diaper bag. Dig it out and get ready to tote Maisy."

Without another word, Lara got busy complying. If he could wipe the sadness from her eyes and ease the tension from her jaw, he'd do it in a heartbeat.

Soon, they came to that dead-end road he'd spotted. He backed the pickup past the entrance to it and then gunned ahead into the tree-crowded route. If the branches had been brushing them before, now metal met wood in groaning squeals. He powered the vehicle over a small fallen log. The bump jounced his head nearly to the roof of the cab. A small cry came from Lara, and Maisy began to fuss.

"Hang on. I see an end in sight. We aren't going to be able to drive much farther."

A moment later, they burst into a small clearing, and the road came to an end. The stone-ringed firepit in the center of the area suggested this was one of the rustic campsites offering no amenities for those who wanted the true backcountry experience.

He stopped the truck at the far edge of the clearing and got out with his backpack and the shotgun. Lara, wearing the infant harness, stepped out her door.

"We shouldn't leave my go bag behind," she said. "I've got some trail snacks in there and even rudimentary fishing equipment that could suffice in a pinch." She slung the bag over her shoulder. "And we'll have to take Maisy's diaper bag and one of those gallon jugs of purified water for her bottles."

"No need for the jug," Ethan told her. "Jake filled all Maisy's bottles with water before he put them in the diaper bag. They're ready for mixing. She should have enough to last a day or two. My backpack has bottled water for us."

"*Prepared* is your middle name."

"Thank Jake. He loaded the stuff."

At the mention of her friend, Lara's gaze shadowed and she looked away. "There's a footpath in that direction." She pointed.

Ethan frowned. "I hate to take an obvious path, but on the other hand, I hate to head into unexplored territory. Who knows what trouble we could get into?"

"How could it be much worse than what's pursuing us? But I vote for taking the human-made path to start with. Maybe an alternate route, like a deer trail, will present itself."

Lara retrieved Maisy from her car seat, and Ethan helped her buckle the child into the harness. The gadget left Lara's hands free while providing comfortable transportation for the baby. Judging by the smile on the little one's face, despite her interrupted nap, Maisy was looking forward to a hike like those she'd gotten used to while they were staying at the cabin.

Ethan started up the footpath. They were heading slightly downhill. It might be a fair guess this trail would lead to a creek or even a small lake. His study of the forest map and their daily walks in the woods had shown him those were common in the area. They might be up against overwhelming numbers in this bid for escape, but they had one big thing going for them.

He looked over his shoulder at Lara, striding free and easy behind him. "If the hired guns behind us are anything like the ones who hunted us at that convenience store, they're not going to be too comfortable in the woods. I was raised hunting and camping in the Great Smoky Mountains of Virginia, and you're something of an expert on the Wyoming wilderness, so we should fare all right."

She shot him a tight smile. "We need any advantage we can get."

"I couldn't agree more."

He glanced behind them, and all appeared peaceful. They might have a small respite. It would take some time for the thugs in that SUV to run on foot the distance Lara, Maisy and he had covered in the truck.

Their little party trekked onward for another ten minutes or so. Ethan kept the shotgun in the crook of his arms, ready for use. There was still no sound of pursuit. Didn't mean there wasn't any—that would be hoping for too much. It just meant the armed thugs weren't close enough to hear.

Maisy was talking soft baby-babble. During their walks, she'd proven herself to be an outdoors aficionado. That was a good thing, because a bawling infant would lead their enemies right to them. They just needed to be sure to keep Maisy happy and quiet, which meant, in a sense, that the smallest and youngest was the boss of their progress.

The forest abruptly ended at the shoreline of a pristine blue lake. Ethan sucked in a breath. It was impossible not to be awed by the sheer beauty around them, despite their dire situation. The water of the small lake was so clear that the mountain looming beyond was reflected in its depths, like a mirror. Wildflowers in vivid shades of red and yellow were strewed in grassy patches around the water, creating a vibrant frame for the tableau.

Lara came up beside him, gaping like he was. "Wow! When I was here before, I never found this location. I have got to come back here sometime and snap some shots and take video."

At her positive words about a happier future, he smiled down at her golden head, and his chest warmed. The view he was looking at this instant was as breathtaking as the lake.

But he couldn't tell her that right now. Maybe never. They needed to move along.

He pulled the forest map out of a pocket of his backpack and spread it out. "I figure our pursuers are probably a good fifteen to twenty minutes behind us. They are likely on foot since their vehicle and Jake's looked fairly wrecked by the collision."

"But they're surely calling in reinforcements." Lara's lips pressed into a thin line.

"No doubt, but those hired guns aren't going to be any closer than the others. As far as I can tell, our current location is here." He placed his finger on a spot that depicted a small lake with a rustic campsite nearby. "Here is the little-used route we took into the area, but there is a better access road on the other side of the lake that may be the direction from which those reinforcements you mentioned will come at us."

"So we take a different way out of here entirely."

"And fast."

Lara turned in a slow one-eighty. "Deer path right there." She pointed toward a spot on the east side of the lake with the barest suggestion of an opening in the woodland undergrowth.

"You're right. There it is. Let's go."

Lara shot him a grin, and Ethan fell into step behind her, gaze sharp as he continually scanned the area for threat. How they were going to escape the net of well-resourced hostiles closing in around them, he had no idea, but Lara or Maisy falling into the hands of Drayton's thugs was beyond unthinkable.

ELEVEN

Lara sang softly to Maisy as they trooped along in the cool shade of the forest canopy. The little girl was growing fussy as time wore on. The nap cut short by the excitement on the road had taken a toll on her disposition. There was no way the child could realize her crying might bring more danger down upon them. Hopefully, Maisy would nod off again soon and wake up happier. Well, once she'd been changed and fed, which was always the first order of business after a nap.

The deer path was rough and strewed with obstacles like fallen limbs and the tops of substantial boulders peeking up from the rich earth, as well as tree branches sticking out to impede and poke them. Lara was careful not to trip or to allow the sharp ends of the branches to scratch Maisy, who sat face-forward in her sling across Lara's chest.

"Let me take point now," Ethan said. "I can clear the way for you. I think we need to pick up the pace. Our pursuers may or may not be able to figure out which way we went, but I don't want to risk any of them catching up to us."

Lara stopped and faced him. "I'd say you're right, if we even knew where we were going. This deer path helps keep us under the radar of those who are hunting us—for now—but we have no idea where the trail will lead. Eventually, we're going to end up in a spot where a human being can go no farther, or else the path will take us to another area where people are. And where there are people, we can assume our enemies will be looking for us, also."

Ethan produced a compass from his pack and consulted it. "From what I remember of the map, if we continue on this trajectory, we should come out very near one of the main campgrounds."

"Right where Drayton's people will be swarming."

"But don't forget law enforcement is also converging on the area. I anticipate a lot of standoffs taking place where the cops can't actually arrest the obvious hard cases, because hanging around a campground or driving through a federal forest is not illegal. But on the other hand, the thugs won't be comfortable sticking around certain areas where the cops are. We could use that tension to our advantage."

"How?"

Her tone emerged sharper than she liked, but they had to have a better plan than slinking around in the forest until the bad guys went away. Maisy would need more formula well before the danger faded. Besides, they had no gear for living indefinitely in the outdoors, and should they get caught in a violent storm without shelter, the results could be disastrous—especially with an infant in tow. Not to mention the very real danger from wild animals like bears or cougars. It was a marvel they hadn't yet seen anything more vicious than a pika, a small rabbit with round ears and no tail.

Ethan cupped Lara's shoulder with a warm hand and tickled Maisy under the chin with the other. "I think we can handle ourselves in the forest until dusk starts to fall. Then I want us to creep in close to a main road. As soon as we spot a law enforcement vehicle, we'll flag it down and let the cops drive us out of here."

"Sounds simple."

Ethan's gaze bored into hers. "I hope it is, but the plan also depends on circumstances lining up to our advantage."

"So we'd best pray. I'll take you up on your offer to lead now." She stepped to the side and motioned him ahead of her.

At least they had a plan, as tenuous as it might be, but it was better than having no idea what to do next. Running and hiding was getting very old. Their surroundings might be incredibly gorgeous, and every breath of fresh air rich with scents of moss and pine, but it was difficult to appreciate nature's attractions when one never knew if the next second might hold a deadly ambush.

They trekked onward for about another ten minutes then Lara called a halt.

"We have to do something with Maisy. Her crying is getting louder."

"Agreed." Ethan set down his pack, propped the shotgun against a tree and then helped Lara undo the straps on the baby harness.

Once freed of the contraption, Lara was able to cuddle the baby and bounce her while speaking in a soothing tone. The fussing eased off a little.

"Would you mix one of those bottles for her?" Lara asked. "It's not time for her next feeding, but it might help settle her down. Maybe even get her to fall asleep again."

A few moments later, Lara perched on a rocky outcropping and eased the nipple into the child's mouth. The crying tapered off and silence dropped like a feather around them. Lara scarcely dared breathe as she listened intently for any human-type noises that would indicate the baby's fussing had led their enemies to them. Ethan also seemed frozen in place except for the swivel of his head as he searched their environment for threats.

Gradually, forest noises made themselves known to Lara's senses... A rustle in the fallen pine needles nearby, probably a mouse. Little chirps and warbles from different species of birds. And the whisper of the wind sifting through the branches of the white-bark pine trees surrounding them.

The tense muscles around her spine began to relax.

Then a pair of sharp reports cracked through the air, distant but distinct, coming from a direction at a right angle to the path they were following. A shiver ran through Lara's body.

"A hunter?" Lara ventured.

"I don't think so." Ethan shook his head. "Sounded like handgun fire to me, not a hunting rifle. Thankfully, the shooter wasn't someone directly behind us on our trail, but that doesn't mean it isn't a party converging on our location from another direction."

"Who or what could they be shooting at?"

"I hope only a wild animal." Ethan shrugged. "Or maybe one of Drayton's big-city crew got spooked by a wilderness noise."

Lara bit her lip against blurting out the possibility she didn't want to consider. Maybe the tension between the cops and the thugs had turned violent. Again. How could she bear more bloodshed in their wake?

"I think we need to go now," Ethan said, scooping up their belongings. "Just carry the baby in your arms and do whatever you can to keep her quiet."

Lara offered a wordless nod and followed on his heels, allowing his bulk to part the branches ahead of them and offer safe passage for Maisy and her. The baby did go back to sleep until they stopped again at noon. They changed her and played with her, then they ate some of the trail snacks from Lara's go bag and drank some of the water from Ethan's backpack.

Soon they were on the trail again, now with Maisy back in her sling. Their route contained very few stretches of level terrain. It was mostly uphill or downhill, sometimes at a fairly steep grade, and Lara gratefully accepted Ethan's steadying hand. Baby-on-board definitely affected her balance, and she didn't care to risk taking a tumble with her precious cargo.

From time to time, other deer paths bisected the one they were on, and Ethan used his compass to select the route that kept them headed roughly for a road where they might find law enforcement vehicles. They also might find enemy transportation, but telling the difference by the markings—or lack thereof—shouldn't be difficult. At least that's what Lara kept telling herself.

Dusk was closing in on them when they finally came upon a road. It wasn't paved, but it was wide and freshly graveled, indicating a main artery through the forest. In silent accord, Lara hunkered down next to Ethan behind the cover of some leafy bushes that concealed their presence while allowing them to observe the road from a few yards upslope.

"If a police or marshals service vehicle comes along," Ethan said quietly in her ear, "let me make the approach and stop them. Only show yourself if I motion you to come."

She turned her head and gazed into his eyes. "And if you don't tell me to come? If there's a problem?"

"You take off and let me handle it. I'll get clear, and I *will* find you."

"But—"

He pressed a finger against her lips. "Trust me."

She grasped his hand and squeezed it. "I do, Ethan. More than anyone else on this planet except for my mother, and you're right up there with her. But I don't know how I'd cope if something happens to you."

The sheer intensity of the declaration from her own mouth took Lara's breath away. Just how deeply was she coming to care for this man? Could this depth of emotion be real? Lasting? Or was it born of the desperation of their situation? How could she know?

His entire countenance softened. "You'd carry on. You're a fighter, Lara. I trust you to do what's right."

Her insides turned to mush. Matt had never said anything remotely like that to her. He'd always encouraged her dependency and highlighted her weaknesses. Why was she continually comparing Ethan to Matt? There *was* no comparison, and it was about time she broke the habit of analyzing men through Matt-colored lenses. Something like an electric shock flowed through Lara. Wasn't that defensive thought process a form of still letting Matt control her? Why had she never seen that simple truth before?

There was no time to examine the stunning self-revelation as vehicle headlights appeared on the road, along with a steady crunch of gravel. A sedan proceeded toward them at a sedate pace. Friend or foe? Both types of people were looking for them.

"It's a county sheriff's vehicle," Ethan hissed urgently in her ear. "I'm going to flag them down."

Lara opened her mouth to acknowledge his message, but he was already gone. His long legs carried him to the verge of the road in a few strides. One arm waved for attention while the other held the shotgun at the ready. The vehicle braked so suddenly to a halt that it skidded on the gravel. Lara's heart lightened as the vehicle door opened and a woman in a uniform hopped out. Something had finally gone right.

"Not a sound!" A voice growled low and menacing behind her as a hard object poked her in the back of the head.

A gun? Lara's brain went woozy as if all the blood had drained from it.

"You're coming with me," the harsh voice continued. "Let's move."

"Lara!" Ethan called up the hill toward the bushes where they had taken cover. "Come on out. It's time to go."

There was no response. His gaze searched the hillside, but gathering dusk hid many details. Where were she and the baby? He called out again, but no answer came.

"Something's wrong," he told the sheriff's deputy, who had introduced herself as Cherise Taylor. "Draw your gun and follow me."

Ethan led the way up the hillside to the bushes. His insides twisted. No one was there. They had to have been taken, which meant that the Draytons had at least one thug on their payroll who knew how to track and how to move silently in the wilderness. He shouldn't be surprised. It was only to be expected that the father and son had reached out to a woodsman in this situation.

How could he find them now with night closing in? But find them—and quickly— he must. The abductor could choose any moment to kill Lara and make off with the baby. The only thing that might have kept him from doing the deed already was the need for stealth and speed to put distance between them and Ethan. That, and he would use Lara as a mule to carry the baby until they reached a safe destination. Safe for the abductor, not for Lara or Maisy.

Ethan quickly and concisely explained the situation to the sheriff's deputy.

"I should call for backup to come to this location," she said.

"Negative. The law will swarm to this spot but so will the bad guys, and we could easily end up with multiple casualties. Pull your car over and shut it off, then rejoin me. I'm going to look for an indication of which way our perp took Lara and the baby."

"Will do," she said. "I'll be on your six as soon as you know which direction to go in."

Keeping the shotgun at the ready, Ethan palmed his flashlight from his utility belt and shined the beam over the surrounding terrain. There! A broken twig testified to recent passage, and farther on, a flower had been crushed by a foot. Clever. The abductor wasn't taking his captives back along the deer path into the interior of the forest. He was moving them parallel to the road just inside the tree line. The objective must be to meet up with a vehicle carrying Drayton muscle.

"Change of plan," he said to the deputy as she came up to him. "The direction Lara and Maisy are being taken tells me the perp has called his friends to come meet them farther up the road. Take your car and keep driving slowly like you were before. I'll stay on the trail here. I'd like to stop the kidnapper by stealth before he reaches his friends, but failing that, you'll be there to back me up if we all converge on the perps' getaway car. We *cannot* allow them to get Lara and Maisy into the vehicle."

"Understood." Cherise jerked a nod.

"Take this with you." Ethan stripped off his backpack and handed it to the deputy. "I don't need the bulk when I'm trying to move quickly and quietly."

Cherise took the pack and loped off toward her vehicle.

Ethan moved on foot as swiftly as he was

able in the gloom, along a slope that got steeper the farther he went. It wouldn't do for him to make a misstep and take a tumble, possibly sprain an ankle or worse. At least he could be assured that the terrain was also slowing Lara and Maisy and their captor. Ethan had turned off his flashlight so as not to betray his position, but he was able to make out trampled grass along the route, assuring him that he was still hot on the scent.

A twig snap and a soft cry close ahead alerted Ethan that he was nearly on top of his quarry. He slowed to a creep, ears straining for further direction.

There!

A growled curse wafted out of the gloom mere paces away. He made out a shadowy figure almost straight ahead of him.

"Move faster!" ordered a harsh whisper.

"Do you want me to go top over tail down this hill with the baby strapped to me?" retorted an indignant female voice.

Ethan used the sound of the conversation to ease closer to the confrontation.

"How about I put a bullet in you right now and take that baby?" the man snarled.

Ethan surged forward and slammed the

butt of his shotgun into the man's head. The abductor crumpled like a rag.

"How about you don't," he said to the unconscious thug.

"Ethan!" Lara cried out.

The next thing he knew, she was in his arms. He hugged her close, but Maisy squawked against being crushed between them and they separated. With one hand, Ethan caressed the infant's downy head, and with the other, he cupped Lara's soft cheek.

She leaned into his palm. "You found us so fast. Thank you!"

"There's no way I was letting you go."

His heart skipped a beat at what he heard his mouth say. Did he mean those words in more than an immediate sense? When this was all over, did he want to explore the possibility of something more permanent with her in his life? He firmed his jaw. Poor time to be asking himself those questions. They needed to put distance between themselves and the bad guys.

The crunch of tires on gravel brought him into a crouching turn. He motioned Lara to remain silent. The vehicle suddenly blipped a siren and flashed its lights.

"Good. It's Deputy Cherise. Let's get out of here before any enemies show up."

Ethan assisted Lara and her precious cargo down the embankment. They soon caught up with the sheriff's vehicle and piled into the back seat. Ethan closed the car door just as another vehicle's lights appeared around a bend ahead and closed on them rapidly.

"Swing a U-turn fast as a yo-yo and blare those lights and the siren. We've got to make a run for it."

"On it." Cherise cranked the wheel even as she accelerated the vehicle.

The car performed a sliding turn, and they blasted up the road in full-pursuit speed— only they were the ones being chased. Maisy, still in her baby harness attached to Lara, reacted to the loud siren by adding her wails to the din. Lara cuddled the child close and attempted in vain to comfort her.

"*Now* call it in," Ethan yelled to the driver. "You can be sure our pursuers are also reaching out for their cronies."

Using hands-free mode, the deputy notified all law enforcement vehicles in the area to converge on their location. The gravel road reached a terminus with a paved highway. Ignoring the stop sign and without slowing, the deputy whipped the vehicle into a rubber-burning, tail-swishing turn onto the larger thoroughfare.

The abrupt change of direction threw Lara into Ethan's shoulder, and she cried out. Maisy's bawling ramped up a notch. Ethan resisted the impulse to wrap his arms around the pair. Sure, he needed to keep them safe, but the hired guns in the SUV nearly riding their bumper were the greater threat. Ethan pumped a load into the barrel of the shotgun.

He glanced over at Lara. "I'm going to take a page out of your book and add my own twist." Then he looked toward the driver. "Roll down my window, please, Cherise." The rear windows of law enforcement vehicles had to be operated by the driver.

The sheriff's deputy complied, and Ethan leaned his torso outside. Humid night air created a slipstream around him. He pointed the shotgun's barrel at the pursuing vehicle's hood and pulled the trigger. Instantly, smoke geysered from the SUV's engine, and the vehicle began swerving all over the road.

"You did it!" Lara cried even as their driver let out a whoop.

Ethan eased back into his seat and Cherise powered up the window.

He blew out a long breath. "Now we keep on driving and see who reaches us first, the good guys or the bad guys."

TWELVE

Would this nightmare never end? Lara shrugged her shoulders out of her bulky go bag, tossed it on the floor and then bounced and snuggled a crying and kicking Maisy.

Moments later, a set of flashing lights zoomed toward them from the other lane ahead. The vehicles passed each other, but the other car did a swift U-turn and came up on them to form a rear guard. Then a second law enforcement vehicle, lights strobing, entered the highway ahead of them from a side road. Now they had a complete escort.

"Can we slow this circus down a little?" she asked Ethan.

"Sorry." He shook his head. "We need to be sure we've broken through whatever drag-net our enemies have spread, as well as pick up another protection vehicle, before I'll feel comfortable doing that."

"I get it." Lara sighed. "But at least can we do without the siren?"

"You heard the lady." He tapped the driver's shoulder, and the din faded away. "Let's douse the bubble lights, too," he added. "Let your people know."

"Roger that," the deputy answered and got on the radio.

As the vivid reds and blues ceased searing her eyes, Lara slumped against her seat. What was causing her hand to start feeling numb? She looked down to find the diaper bag strap twisted around her wrist. In all the excitement, she'd hung on to Maisy's tote—or, rather, the tote had hung on to *her*. She dug out the baby's pacifier, and the child immediately settled down.

A rumble began to draw near overhead. Helicopter? Lara exchanged a glance with Ethan. Friend or foe?

The ringtone on Ethan's burner cell began to play. Frowning, he pulled the item out of his shirt pocket and stared at the screen. Lara's insides clenched like a fist.

Ethan tapped the screen. "Partner?"

"I'm in the chopper overhead—" Terry's voice came out of the speaker "—along with a couple of our best sharpshooters. Anyone from Drayton's crew tries to get close, and we'll take them out."

The breath Lara had been holding gusted out. Friend. Finally.

"Welcome to the party, buddy," Ethan said with a laugh.

"We'll keep you company all the way to Cheyenne," Terry answered. "Along with your vehicle escorts. I don't know what your status is in that car down there, but unless someone is injured, we don't recommend you stop anywhere until we arrive at our destination."

Lara leaned toward the phone. "We're all right, Terry. Thank God!"

"Amen to that," Ethan added. "Little Maisy is pristine, and Lara and I collected nothing but minor scrapes and bumps during our flight through the forest. No thanks to the goon squad trying its best to take us out."

"Speaking of goons," Terry said, "we arrested a few this afternoon who were getting out of line with forest staff and patrons. One of them even exchanged gunfire with a ranger."

"That must have been the shots we heard this afternoon," Ethan said.

"Likely."

"Was anyone hurt?" Lara put in.

"The ranger winged the attacker."

"What about my friend Jake?" Lara asked, heart beating a little faster.

"Is that the ranger who put his truck in the path of an SUV full of the hard cases who tried to attack you on the road?"

"That's the one."

"I'm told he's in the hospital for observation. Suspected mild concussion from the collision, but I hear he's doing fine."

Lara smiled at Ethan, and he reached over and grasped her hand. She gladly left it resting in his possession.

"I'm putting that guy's name in for a commendation, for sure," Ethan said, "and Deputy Cherise behind the wheel here deserves some sort of expert-driving award."

The woman up front laughed and gave them a backhanded wave. "Think nothing of it. My privilege."

"How is my mother doing?" Lara asked Terry.

"Fine and feisty at last check-in," he answered.

"Sounds like my mom." A giggle escaped her throat. The tone was a bit high and giddy, but relief after a long day of terror had that effect on a person's vocal cords.

"How are we doing on the hunt for Ronnie and Vinnie?" Ethan asked.

"We're currently squeezing every drop of intel out of those thugs we arrested today. I'll let you know what we find out."

"Do that." Ethan ended the call and turned his head toward Lara.

She met his gaze with a stern stare. "I'm praying we catch a break because we can't go on being chased like sheep. I won't do this anymore. We have to settle on a plan, no matter what the danger."

"You mean some version of the scenarios we've been discussing where you feature as the lamb staked out as bait and the Draytons come to us?"

"Yes, one of those plans. And don't worry, I can shed my wool in a hurry when it's time to get fierce."

"Don't I know it. But what we haven't come up with yet is some ploy that doesn't smell like a trap to bring the Draytons themselves out of the woodwork."

Lara pressed her lips together and turned her head away. Always, those vital details had been sticking points in their discussions.

She agreed that being used as bait would be a pointless exercise unless there was a strong probability of drawing out the father-son team behind all this mayhem. However, she didn't have a solution to the problem.

God, help us see our way. The simple, desperate prayer was the best Lara could muster.

Ethan gently deposited a sleeping Maisy in the play pen bought for her use in the Wyoming headquarters of the US Marshals Service and stood quietly observing the child's utter relaxation. The infant was the embodiment of innocent sweetness and ought to be raised in an atmosphere of loving kindness and integrity. Bottom line: both Maisy and Lara deserved to be happy and safe and Ethan *had* to give them that opportunity. Failure was not an option.

Firming his jaw, he left the small office that had been set up as a temporary nursery and joined Lara in the staff break room. Savory scents wafted from takeout containers sitting on the table. Ethan's stomach rumbled, reminding him he hadn't eaten anything since he and Lara had inhaled energy bars while they'd been on the run in the forest.

Lara saluted him with the chopsticks she

was using to scoop food into her mouth from one of the containers. "Kung pao chicken. My favorite. I think there's beef and broccoli, sweet-and-sour pork and pot stickers in these other containers."

Ethan grabbed the beef and broccoli and settled across from her. "Maisy's down for the count, I think."

"That's good. I don't believe I'll be far behind her." A yawn smothered against her wrist punctuated her words.

"Food and rest are probably the best things right now. You can sleep secure. Armed guards are stationed all over this building. Tomorrow, we can think things through with fresh minds."

She sent him a mild frown. "I'm okay with that answer for tonight, but we need to have some serious discussions tomorrow and make decisions. If running and hiding, then being found and running and hiding again is your version of playing it safe, I'm all for taking some risk by going on the offensive, as long as Maisy isn't a part of the plan."

Ethan bottled a sigh. She was right about needing to make decisions but wrong that taking a greater risk was the only option. Now was not the time to explain the play-it-safe alternative, though. By now he knew Lara well enough to anticipate she wasn't going to like the idea going through his mind. But for this moment, the better part of wisdom was devoting himself quietly to his Chinese takeout.

An hour later, Lara had retired to her cot in the same office where Maisy was sleeping, and Ethan was still in the break room nursing the dregs of a cup of tea. Soon, he would seek out one of the cots that had been set up for him and Terry in another office. This was truly a temporary arrangement because they couldn't go on disrupting HQ functionality indefinitely. But at least for now, he was thankful for a safe sanctuary, however temporary it might be.

Ethan rose and rinsed his cup in the sink. He turned to find Terry sauntering into the room…cradling Maisy? No, it was a baby doll that resembled the real infant. The limbs were even soft and loose, like a human baby's arms and legs.

"Playing with dolls now, are we?" Ethan let out a soft chuckle. "Or maybe it's your bedtime teddy bear substitute."

"Very funny." His partner shot him a mock scowl. "No, I went to the mall and bought this while you and Lara were eating."

"What for? Maisy's too small to play with it."

Terry grabbed a bottled water out of the fridge, turned and closed the door with his foot. "While you were being all fatherly by feeding, changing and putting Maisy to bed, I had a long chat with Lara. She told me you've been brainstorming plans to draw the Draytons out of hiding by using her as bait. All versions of the idea require a doll that resembles Maisy enough to be mistaken for her at a distance, so I got started rounding up the props."

Ethan crossed his arms over his chest and shook his head. "I'm going to have to nix those plans. Every version of the bait scenario is too dangerous. Besides, we haven't come up with one that assures us Vinnie and Ronnie will show up in person. If *we* initiate something, they'll smell a trap a mile away and not show up."

"Then we need to keep on brainstorming. There are a lot of sharp minds in this office."

"I'm game for continuing to bounce ideas around, but I'm not hopeful we'll come up with a scenario Lara and I haven't already discussed." Ethan spread his hands with a shrug. "I mean, how would we let Vinnie and Ronnie know where Lara's going to be at any given time without making it obvious we're laying a trap?"

"If we even figure out how to contact them in the first place." Terry set the doll on the table and twisted open the cap on his bottle.

"Right. And Lara can't just pop up into the open somewhere and hope the Draytons will come running. They'll only send more hired thugs, and we'll be back on the same run-and-hide treadmill."

"Back to square one with no progress." Terry took a swig of his water. "You're thinking permanent witness protection, then?"

"New identity. The whole nine yards. At least until we succeed in bringing down this vicious father-son team."

"But who knows how long that will take."

"Exactly, which is why we need to settle Lara and Maisy in somewhere for the long haul. I think Marshal Teague will go for the idea as long as Lara is on board to testify to everything the Draytons put her through."

Ethan ignored the wrench in his gut at what this long-haul scenario would mean for him. Lara and Maisy would be taken as far out of range of Drayton influence as possible— somewhere the crooks wouldn't have eyes and ears. And Ethan couldn't be allowed to know where that was. Nor would he ever be able to go near them, because he was now a known associate of theirs. To save them, he'd have to give them up.

But he was prepared to make the sacrifice. Their survival was more important than seeking his own happiness by pursuing a relationship with Lara. Even though they might never be together, it was about time he admitted to himself that he truly *wanted* that relationship. More than anything except her and Maisy's safety.

"Earth to Ethan," Terry said, waving a hand in his face.

"Huh?" Ethan took a step backward.

"You went somewhere, buddy, but don't worry, I get it. I see how you two look at each other." The warm compassion in Terry's eyes sent thickness to Ethan's throat.

"Let's hit the sack," he said, voice a little raspy. "Tomorrow's another day."

Quite likely the day he'd say goodbye to beautiful Lara and precious Maisy. If he'd needed another lesson about the dangers of developing personal feelings for those he was protecting, he was receiving it now. A lesson he'd never forget. Just like he'd never forget the pair who'd stolen his heart.

THIRTEEN

Lara woke up with a start and sat up. Where was she? Odors of ink and paper mixed with fruity air freshener tweaked her nostrils. She scanned her surroundings in the pale light filtering between the window blinds. An office? Oh, that's right. They were at the Wyoming US Marshals Service headquarters in the US District Court building in Cheyenne, and they were safe for the time being. Tension ebbed from her shoulder muscles.

Judging from the soft rustles and mewls coming from the play yard in the corner, Maisy was working herself awake, which meant the time was likely around six. Lara stood up from the cot, which had turned out to be more comfortable than she'd expected. Or maybe she'd just been so tired she wouldn't have noticed if it had been a bed of nails.

Clad in the modest and comfy pajamas

she'd donned last night from her go bag, she padded barefoot into the hallway on her way to the break room to prepare Maisy's bottle. This early, the day staff hadn't come into the office for work yet. A sense of quiet emptiness blanketed the area. However, an armed guard near the elevator offered her a nod and a quick good morning. She gave the man a smile and replied in kind.

As she neared her destination, the odor of fresh coffee greeted her, as well as the sound of men's voices wrapped in conversation. From the intense tones, the discussion was urgent. Her stomach clenched. What was going on *now*?

Stepping into the room, she found both Ethan and Terry seated at the table, steaming mugs of brew in front of them. Their talking abruptly ceased. Wearing pasted-on smiles, both men swiveled their heads toward her. Unless she was greatly mistaken, the subject of their conversation had been her—or more likely, her and Maisy. The men offered her synchronized good mornings.

Lara put her hands on her hips and frowned at them. "If ever I've seen a pair of culprits guilty of something, it's you two. What is it I'm not going to be happy about?"

Terry looked at Ethan. "Is she this way all the time?"

"Welcome to my world, pal. She sizes up a situation in nothing flat and calls it like she sees it."

"It's not something to do with my mom?" Lara's heart took up residence in her throat.

"No, nothing like that." Ethan took a sip from his mug and quirked a brow at her. "If a situation involving your mother had come to our attention, we would have woken you up."

Lara sniffed. The man was back to using a formal tone and diction again when addressing her. What did *that* mean?

"Never mind, then." She headed for the bottle-making supplies on the counter. "I don't want to know. Yet." She turned and sent a stern stare toward Ethan and his partner. "Let me get Maisy fed, changed and settled first. *Then* we'll have a heart-to-heart."

"Agreed," Ethan said.

"We'll hang right here." Terry saluted her with his mug.

Ethan's sober gaze upon her while she made the bottle did nothing to ease the jumpiness in her middle. Whatever it was must be as problematic as it came. Of course, everything about this current situation was beyond serious.

Lara returned to the office-cum-bedroom that she occupied with the baby. Maisy was fully awake and starting to bawl and kick for her breakfast.

"There now, sweet pea," she said as she scooped the fussing baby up.

Her attachment to Maisy had grown exponentially each day, but was she setting herself up for incredible heartache? If Izzy was still alive, if this nightmare ever came to an end with the Draytons apprehended, the baby's birth mother would certainly reclaim her. That was the best-case scenario. Right?

Best for Maisy, probably, but devastating for Lara. What an emotional paradox she found herself in. She wanted her friend to be all right and to be able to raise her child, and yet she didn't want to have to say good-bye to Maisy. Someone was slated for heartache. The mess appeared to have no solution that made everyone happy, any more than there appeared to be a solution to laying a trap for the Draytons that guaranteed everyone's safety.

As she cuddled Maisy, Lara pushed the troubling thoughts away, though they lurked in the shadows of her mind. Thankfully, caring for the baby offered an effective distraction from obsessing over problems with no easy answers. The little girl was in a great mood this morning, smiling and cooing even while attempting to drink from her bottle. The cute antics offered Lara an opportunity to laugh. But the idyll eventually came to an end.

Lara deposited Maisy in her infant seat and then changed into a pair of jeans and a T-shirt and donned her sneakers. She took Maisy across the hall to the ladies' room and handled necessities, including brushing her hair. Then, steeling herself for whatever hard discussion awaited, she and Maisy headed for the break room.

Early bird day staffers were starting to arrive at the courthouse. Her progress was slowed by people greeting her and baby-talking to Maisy and making funny faces. Size, age or gender didn't seem to matter when encountering an infant. The biggest and toughest looking got as goofy as the dainty and delicate. The phenomenon would be amusing if she wasn't on pins and needles to rejoin Ethan and Terry. At last, she entered the break room, but the place was empty.

Lara let out a humph. "So much for hanging right here."

She set the baby seat on the table and poured herself a cup of coffee. A doll perched on the counter against a nearby wall. Lara picked it up. It was soft and lifelike and bore a distinct resemblance to Maisy. Her breathing hitched. Maybe Ethan and Terry had come up with a scenario to trap the Draytons after all. Did she dare hope?

She set down the doll and took a sip of her coffee. Her stomach rumbled, reminding her that Maisy wasn't the only one who liked to eat in the morning.

"Breakfast is served." Terry's cheerful voice drew her attention.

"You read my mind." She glanced around, but Ethan wasn't entering in his partner's wake. "Where's your sidekick?"

"Sidekick? Sounds good to me." Terry grinned at her as he set foam containers on the break table. "But don't tell Ethan I said that."

He promptly began to make goofy faces at Maisy and speak baby talk to her. The infant responded with smiles and fist waves.

Lara shook her head. Yup. Definitely a universal phenomenon. Not that she could blame anyone for going a little gaga over Miss Adorbs when she was a total goner herself.

"So, where *is* Deputy Ridgeway?" She deliberately formalized her tone.

Terry chuckled and motioned for her to take a seat at the table. "I see you noticed his reversion to being buttoned-up. He's in with the marshal now."

"Discussing options? I thought you were going to talk to *me* first."

Terry shook his head. "Not when he's summoned by the man himself."

"Okay, I suppose I'll have to wait until he shows up to find out what you guys are thinking?" She made the statement into a question. "A plan to capture the Draytons, maybe?"

Terry just shrugged and pushed a foam container over in front of her. "Eat your breakfast."

Despite the savory bacon-and-egg odors wafting to her nose, Lara's appetite waned. Something wasn't right if Terry didn't want to say a word without Ethan present. She picked at her food and finally managed to wash down a slice of bacon wrapped in a piece of toast with her coffee. Meanwhile, Maisy continued to draw office workers who popped in to grab a coffee and lingered awhile to make googly eyes at the baby.

At last, Ethan walked in like a breath of doom and gloom, his expression a cross between a scowl and a glare. His gaze landed on Maisy and his expression brightened. He took a seat opposite Lara and kitty-corner from Terry.

"Sorry to keep you waiting."

"Couldn't be helped," she answered. "I hear you were called into your boss's office."

Ethan grimaced. "My fault, I guess. I left him a message last night that I needed to speak to him first thing in the morning. Marshal Teague took me at my word, and I'd say that's a good thing. We've already got the ball rolling."

"What ball, exactly?" Lara narrowed her eyes at Ethan.

He sighed and exchanged a glance with Terry, then returned his gaze to her. "We've come to the conclusion that placing you and Maisy in the WITSEC program is the safest and best option remaining to us."

Lara's mouth went dry. "You mean we'll be moved to the backside of nowhere and given new identities?"

One side of Ethan's mouth quirked upward,

but his gaze remained flat. "We do have nicer places than the backside of nowhere for relocation sites."

"I don't care. This is a terrible idea. I hate it!"

"Me, too." An emotion flickered behind his eyes.

What was he feeling? Was he sad? Glad? Eager to move on to the next assignment?

"What about my mother?" Her pulse fluttered. "I can't leave her."

Terry sat forward and touched her arm. "That's understandable, but I don't know—"

"Given that she's been threatened, also," Ethan interrupted, "she can come with you. I've cleared that with the marshal. But when we get either or both of the Draytons into custody—and we will—you'll be expected to testify about everything you've experienced at the hands of their hired muscle. The testimony will be pertinent because we *do* have financial-transaction evidence that proves they work for the Draytons."

"Of course, I'll be happy to testify. Anything that will get these people taken out of society."

"Then we move forward with the plan."

Lara's chest went hollow, as if all the air

had been sucked from her lungs, leaving a vacuum behind. Was this really going to happen? The life she'd built was being ripped away just like that? Who would she become?

Maisy's mother.

As if someone flipped a light switch, a shameful hope dawned. Shameful because they still didn't know Izzy's fate, whether she was alive or dead. But once the infant went into WITSEC with Lara, would Isabelle be able to reclaim her? Or would Maisy be Lara's forever? An electric thrill ran through her, then her stomach plummeted.

"I can't do it." She drew herself up straight. "A selfish part of me wants to disappear with Maisy, but I can't steal Izzy's child away if my friend is still alive."

Terry frowned. "I think we're at the point of no better choice."

Stillness fell and then Ethan broke it by rising and refilling everyone's coffee cups.

He settled back into his seat and met Lara's gaze. "Clearly, Isabelle Drayton has faced the very real possibility of giving up her daughter for Maisy's best good. Those documents she left with you prove that. We believe it likely that, if she is still alive, she has chosen to disappear herself, which is easier to do on her own, without an infant in tow."

The backs of Lara's eyes stung, and she blinked rapidly. "Okay, I can see that." Her voice rasped. "How soon will this relocation take place?"

"In a few days, and that's fast. It takes a little time to set these things up."

"Then maybe the Draytons will be captured before it happens." If only she felt a molecule of hope that this wish could come true, but these evil people had remained hidden despite a massive manhunt.

"Possibly," Terry said. His voice contained little conviction.

"Reed!" someone called from the doorway of the break room. "The marshal wants to see you."

Terry rose. "Catch you later," he said and left the room.

Lara set her gaze on Ethan. "Will you be accompanying us on this trek into obscurity?"

A faint smile crossed his lips. "Trek into obscurity? Clever way of putting it. Since my association with you is known to the Draytons, I won't be included in your relocation detail or know where you're going."

"But if the Draytons are apprehended and convicted some time down the road, Maisy, my mother and I will be able to come out of hiding, right?"

"Correct."

"But if they're not captured, I won't see you again."

A muscle flexed in Ethan's jaw. "No. Never again. But we'll catch them, believe me."

If only she could fully trust those words, but these evil people had been utterly elusive so far. Lara's heart shattered. When had her vision of a perfect family become Ethan, Maisy and her together? Now that dream was gone before she'd even realized it was there.

On an office computer, Ethan devoted himself to typing his report of all that had occurred since escorting Lara and Maisy from her home in Jackson. He'd made notes when they were at the cabin in Bridger-Teton National Forest, but fleshing out the account served to focus his thoughts away from the impending separation from the pair who had crept past his guard and captured his heart. If only the distraction were more effective.

The devastation in Lara's expression when she was informed of the necessary WITSEC solution kept appearing in Ethan's mind. Was she shattered because her former life was about to be erased? That kind of prospect would turn anyone inside out. Or could there be an additional reason? Why had she asked specifically if she would ever see him again? Did he dare hope she felt something for him besides gratitude for his protection services or the friendship that had developed between them at the cabin? But even if he allowed himself to entertain the idea, such hope was empty in the end. Lara and Maisy needed to disappear, and he needed to let them.

Didn't he?

What if he went into WITSEC with them? Ethan shook his head and jabbed his finger on the enter key more forcefully than necessary. What kind of foolishness was that? He wasn't ready to give up his career. Was he? But if he did make that move, he'd want to be more to her than her protector or friend. Yet asking her about her feelings for him when they were in this emotionally tense situation would be beyond unethical, if not downright cruel. No, they were stuck on separate paths, and he needed to make peace with the facts. If only peace were anywhere to be found in the turmoil within him.

"Ethan?" Lara's voice drew his head up. She was standing in the doorway with Maisy in her arms. "I'm not bothering you at a bad time, am I?"

"Not at all." He rolled his chair away from the desk. "I need a break from staring at this screen before I go cross-eyed."

The wry remark brought a faint smile from Lara, and the sound of his voice attracted Maisy's attention. The baby gazed at him and flapped her little arm. It was his imagination, of course, but the action almost seemed like she was waving at him. Ethan rose and reached for Maisy, and she came readily. The smile he received from the little girl was *not* imaginary.

"She likes you a lot." Lara crossed her arms and leaned into the doorjamb.

"The feeling is mutual." Ethan tickled the little girl's chin and won a chortle in response.

"Good." Lara grinned. Her gaze fell toward his desk, and she pointed at something. "Is that the tracker we found inside the baby rattle?"

Ethan turned and gazed down at the small rectangular black box sitting on the corner of his borrowed desk. "That's the one. Attempting to find the purchaser through the serial number was a dead end, though."

Lara frowned, shook her head and then brightened. "I've been offered an opportunity to shower in the locker room in the basement, and I was hoping you'd look after Maisy."

He fixed Lara with a pointed stare. "The entire building is secure, but you're not leaving this floor unaccompanied."

"Of course not, worry wart. A pair of female Cheyenne PD officers will be with me."

Ethan's shoulders relaxed marginally. "All righty, then. You've got yourself a babysitter. Isn't that right, Maisy-Daisy?" He bounced the little girl in his arms and grinned at her.

"You'll make a great daddy one day," Lara said and walked away.

Ethan stared at the empty doorway. Was that wistfulness he'd heard in her tone, or was his imagination working overtime? He couldn't trust his discernment when his emotions were all over the place.

Get your head together, Ridgeway. Until Lara and Maisy were whisked quietly and secretly away from this location to their new home, he was ultimately responsible for keeping this little one and her guardian safe.

Half an hour later, he'd fed and changed

Maisy, then laid her down for a nap. He stepped into another room, got on the walkie-talkie and called down to one of the PD officers guarding Lara.

"What's the status?" he asked.

"Quiet as a tomb down here."

Ethan winced at the officer's choice of terminology. "Do you have eyes on Lara?"

"No, but I heard the shower shut off a few minutes ago. She's probably getting dressed and applying her makeup."

"Lara doesn't wear makeup." Another reason to marvel at the woman's extraordinary beauty. She had no need to enhance it. "Stay alert. The people after her are very determined and resourceful."

"Copy that."

Another twenty minutes passed, and Ethan got on the radio again. When neither officer answered his calls for response, his hair stood on end. He grabbed a passing deputy and assigned him to Maisy, then strode up the hall and found Terry in another office.

"Lara's guard detail isn't answering from the locker room," he said.

Terry jumped up. "Let's go."

In tandem, they raced toward the elevator.

Ethan's finger stabbed the elevator button just as an alarm started blaring.

"Fire?" Terry's gaze collided with Ethan's.

"Not hardly. This is to disable the elevators and create confusion. The stairs. Let's go!"

Ethan rammed through the stairway door, and his feet carried him downward recklessly fast. The area was soon jammed with people attempting to leave the building. Heart rate revving into overdrive, he muscled his way downward with Terry in his wake. The last length of stairwell, the one leading into the basement, was empty. No one was coming upward to escape the building—not even Lara or her escorts, unless they'd already made it to the first floor. But Ethan couldn't afford to make that assumption, not when the PD officers had failed to respond to his radio call.

Something bad was going on, and he had to stop it before Lara got hurt. If he wasn't already too late.

The alarm continued to blare as they reached the bottom of the stairwell and faced the entrance to the basement hallway. Fighting the urge to keep from heedlessly bursting through the door that very second, Ethan took a position to one side of the entrance, and Terry flattened his back against the wall on the other side. At Terry's nod, Ethan pulled the hydraulic-hinged door open and flung himself through it, posture low and collected, weapon extended.

The fluorescent lights overhead illuminated a long hallway with doors leading this way and that. No sign of armed enemies. No sign of people at all except for a pair of uniformed figures crumpled on the floor at the end of the hall. Ethan's throat tightened. Moving ahead, with Terry on his six, Ethan checked the first room along the route.

"Clear."

Terry moved ahead and checked the next door.

"Clear."

Then Ethan took the next room.

"Clear."

Finally, Terry took the fourth room and pronounced it clear.

Ethan hurried ahead to the pair of officers on the floor. No blood or signs of injury. He touched their necks and found healthy pulses. What had caused them to collapse and lose consciousness?

The entrance to the locker room was closed, and no sounds emanated from within. Heart hammering, Ethan slowly pushed the door open and entered in a shooter's stance. No hostiles evident, though the banks of lockers could hide many thugs. Over the din of the fire alarm, it was impossible to hear any movements enemies might be making. Terry came up beside him, moving his gaze and his gun barrel this way and that.

"Lara?" Ethan called out.

No response.

If anything had happened to her—no, he couldn't think that way. Not right now. The blare of the alarm suddenly cut out. Silence rang in the wake of the clamor. Wordlessly, Ethan canted his head at Terry, who moved off toward one end of the room while Ethan took the other.

"Lara?" Ethan called softly as he rounded the corner into a lane between banks of lockers.

A petite figure dressed in jeans and a T-shirt lay on the floor, prone and still, her still-damp hair a golden curtain across her face.

"Lara!"

FOURTEEN

One side of Lara's jaw and ear throbbed. The other side was pressed against something chilly and hard. Her whole body ached.

"Lara!"

Someone was calling her name. She released a low moan and opened her eyes. Between strands of her hair, squares of black-and-white linoleum swam into view. Her stomach rolled at the chemical odor of wax. What was she doing on the floor?

A pair of booted feet showed up in front of her eyes and then a pair of knees clad in black slacks took their place as someone knelt beside her. Gentle hands moved the hair draped over her face. A face lowered near her own. Ethan!

She started to smile but her jaw protested the movement. "What happened?" she managed to mumble.

"You came down to the locker room to get a shower and someone must have attacked you."

Lara blinked. "I don't..." She was about to say "remember" when it all rushed back to her. "Yes." She began to lever herself off the floor on rubbery arms.

"Whoa, whoa, whoa!" Ethan lifted her up and pulled her close, supporting her against his chest. His heartbeat thrummed in her ear, fast but steady. "We need to get you checked out by a doctor before you get too rambunctious."

"I'm okay, Ethan. At least I will be." She failed to follow up the declaration by pulling away from his warm embrace. Chalk it up to the weakness permeating her body...or simply the comfort of his closeness. "I was just tying my shoes when I heard a small outcry from the hallway. I got up to investigate, but a figure dressed all in black rushed at me, kicked me in the head, and the lights went out."

Terry came around the corner of the bank of lockers and walked up to them. "Lara's okay?"

"She says she will be," Ethan answered.

"Good." The man heaved out a long breath.

"Somebody with martial arts skills kicked her and knocked her out," Ethan continued. "Sounds like Blaine Roberts to me."

"Who's Blaine Roberts?" Lara asked.

Ethan's lips flattened. "The Draytons have this martial arts expert on their payroll."

"Sounds like Roberts took out the officers in the hallway, too. They're up but are still pretty incoherent. One of them mumbled something about being attacked from above. Makes sense since the grate from the air duct above the guards' heads is missing."

"The air ducts? That's how he got in? Roberts is slender enough to make that work."

"That guy is deadly." Terry scowled and planted his hands on his hips. "He can kill with a single blow."

"So why am I still alive?" Lara asked, looking from Ethan to Terry and back again.

"Good question," Ethan said. "We'll pick up that train of thought as soon as we get everyone some medical attention."

"I've radioed for help," Terry said, "but I guess it's still pandemonium upstairs and outside. The fire department is checking the building from top to bottom."

"Why? What happened?" Lara pulled away from Ethan.

"The fire alarm went off," Ethan said. "And I find the timing suspicious."

A shiver ran through Lara. "Where's Maisy?"

Terry jerked a nod toward his partner. "I'll go check while you look after Lara." The man darted out of the room.

"I'm going, too." Lara struggled to get to her feet.

Ethan reached out a hand to help her. Lara gripped his arm but released it as soon as she was upright.

"I have to find her," she told him, and their gazes locked. She refused to look away.

"I know, but you're going to stick to me like glue and let me help you every step of the way."

"No argument from me." A newborn kitten would probably feel less wobbly than she did.

Lara leaned into him as they made their way up the hallway toward the stairwell. The recovering officers formed a rear guard. As they neared the top of the first flight of stairs, Terry burst through the door in front of them.

"Maisy's all right!" he called breathlessly.

Lara's knees went weak, and Ethan lowered her onto a step and squatted beside her.

He looked up at his partner. "They didn't go after her?"

"Sure, they did. As soon as they brought her out during the evacuation. But the marshal had so many officers and deputies around her, they couldn't get close. Our people spotted them and took them down well before they got within reach of her. They're in custody, and hopefully, they have more information than the other Drayton muscle we've apprehended."

Lara looked at Ethan. "The Draytons must be beyond desperate to attempt a stunt like this. Something doesn't add up. It seems staged."

A deep furrow appeared between Ethan's brows. "I agree. What's the theater all about?"

"And I still don't get why my attacker didn't just kill me instead of knocking me out."

"I don't get it either, but I'm glad you're with us." His words were positive, but if his frown got any darker, a storm cloud might form over his head.

An hour later, Lara had been seen by the physician on call with the marshals service. Aside from treating her injuries, the top-to-bottom examination was also designed to look for anything this Blaine Roberts might have planted on her in lieu of killing her. Nothing was found. The doctor diagnosed a bruised jaw, but no break, and a slight concussion. She'd wanted Lara to come in for a CT scan to rule out a subdural hematoma, but Lara had refused and the marshal concurred taking her off premises was too risky.

"Despite the morning's events," Ethan told her as he walked her back to the office she and Maisy had slept in, "this building is still the best place for both of you until we can finalize arrangements for your safe future."

What safe future? Lara didn't voice the question out loud, but it reverberated through her head. If the marshals service hadn't managed to keep her off the Drayton's radar over the past harrowing days, despite Ethan's heroic efforts, what made them think they could pull it off permanently? This was beginning to seem like a losing battle. Maybe it was the head trauma talking, but maybe it was simply facing reality.

Maisy's mewling cry carried up the hallway, and Lara hurried into their shared space. The infant was fussing in the arms of a pacing and harried-looking desk clerk. Lara took the child, and she instantly stopped crying and cuddled up on Lara's shoulder. Warmth flowed through Lara's body. Maisy not only recognized her but needed her. This must be what motherhood felt like. All that afternoon, Lara reveled in the experience like she never had before. When Maisy went down for the night, there was almost a sense of letdown.

As she went to freshen up in the ladies' room and prepare for bed herself, heaviness gripped the pit of Lara's stomach. Ethan had been gone since early afternoon following a lead on the Draytons, and he was still gone. Terry had been scarce, too, though she'd seen him over a shared pizza at supper. Then he'd taken off, as well, presumably to assist Ethan with whatever he was doing. Maisy and she were left under the watchful care of multiple armed guards.

All day long, everyone around had been super nice to her and Maisy, but if she missed Ethan this dearly for one afternoon and evening, adjusting to his absence forever was going to be horrible. She might as well face that her attachment to him was deeper than dependency on him for protection. Here she was surrounded by armed and trained people committed to keeping her safe, and she was still pining. No, her heart longed for Ethan, the man, not the deputy marshal. What a fine mess her emotions were in! And she didn't dare breathe a word of her feelings to Ethan and make things harder than they already were.

Lara plodded back to her cot and sat down on it. The headache that had receded for most of the day had returned with a vengeance. She rubbed the side of her jaw and winced. The tenderness and slight puffiness testified to the purplish bruise she'd seen in the bathroom mirror when she brushed her teeth. Vincent and Ronald Drayton had so much to answer for. When would they finally be brought to justice?

A muffled ringtone sounded from somewhere nearby. Lara jerked and stared toward the landline phone on the desk that had been pushed against the wall to make room for Maisy and her, but that wasn't the source of the ringing. No, the faint sound was coming from…her go bag!

Pulse rate ramping up, Lara unzipped a side pocket of the bag. A cheap burner phone lay within, along with a brown-tinted glass vial containing something liquid. The items had to have been planted in her bag during the fire alarm, perhaps by the same person who had attacked her in the locker room. This

Blaine Roberts person could have crept into this room through the ductwork just as he had done in the basement. With shaking fingers, Lara pulled out the phone and stared at it. No caller ID, but she had no doubt who was trying to communicate and whatever they had to say couldn't be good.

She should run straight to Ethan with this. No, he wasn't back in the office yet. She could go to Terry. No, ditto. What if this call had something to do with Ethan? Her heart seized. Maybe he hadn't returned to the office because he couldn't. Maybe the Draytons had him!

Lara punched the button to answer the call. "Hello?" Her voice came out tentative and trembly. Not at all her normal tone.

"Ms. Werth, good to finally speak with you." She recognized Vincent Drayton's smooth, smarmy voice from the man's brief conversation with Ethan when they were on the run from the bombed safe house.

Something like a fist clenched beneath her breastbone. "I can't say the same thing about you." At least her words came out less wimpy this time.

"Understandable, but in the absence of Deputy Ridgeway and his partner, I believe we can come to a satisfactory arrangement that will spare you unnecessary grief."

"Grief? Have you got Ethan?"

"Why would you think so? Ah, you have feelings for the man. Interesting." The ruthless gunrunner drawled out the last word in a way that ran fingernails across the chalkboard of her mind. "No, but we do have eyes on your mother. Don't worry," he added hastily, "she's still in the custody of the marshals service, but we have a sniper perched nearby, who will take her out at my word."

A slow burn began deep inside Lara. Who did this man think he was, going around threatening innocent people's lives?

"How do I know you're telling the truth?" Her voice had graduated to a snarl.

"Check your text messages. I'll wait."

Lara put the call on hold and brought up the one message that was waiting. It was a photo of her mother walking up to a house Lara didn't recognize, flanked by two men with guns strapped to their sides. The photo was time-stamped from only a couple of hours ago. The Draytons *did* have eyes on her mother. Lara's heart fluttered, then plunged into a gallop.

She returned to the call. "What do you want?" As if she didn't know.

Her world now balanced on a pinpoint of decision. Her mother or Maisy—how could she possibly choose?

Ethan stormed through the door of the marshal's office with Terry on his heels. The marshal had been called about the situation and was on his way in but hadn't arrived yet. The room held a trio of CPD officers who had been standing guard on this floor of the courthouse.

"What happened?" he demanded.

One of the officers was seated, rubbing his head while meeting his gaze with bleary eyes. "I was guarding the elevator. Ms. Werth brought me a cup of coffee. I drank it, and a little while later, it was lights out. When Mitch here—" he waved toward one of the other officers "—found me slumped on the floor and woke me up, we discovered she was gone."

Ethan's stomach twisted. "Lara drugged you and she's missing?"

This couldn't be happening again—betrayal by someone he was protecting. Not

Lara! She wouldn't do that. Would she? A deep burn began under his breastbone.

"We alerted all the night guards immediately," said another officer. "We've searched the building, and she's not on the premises."

"What about Maisy?"

"She's here," said the fourth CPD officer on duty as she entered the room cradling the infant, who was mewling slightly at having her night's sleep disturbed.

Thank You, Lord. Maisy was safe. Wherever Lara had gone, she hadn't taken the baby. But where was she? Why had she left? Even more immediately pertinent, *when* had she left?

"How long ago did Lara give you the coffee?" he asked the officer who'd been stationed at the elevator.

The man glanced up at the wall clock. "Probably an hour ago or thereabouts."

Ethan furrowed his brow. "Say it took ten or twenty minutes for whatever was in there to take effect, she can't have slipped away more than forty minutes ago. Everyone spread out and search this floor with a fine-tooth comb for any clues as to Lara's destination." He turned toward Terry. "See if you can get in touch with someone in tech support to pull the camera footage throughout the building for the past hour."

"On it." Terry walked away, poking at his cell screen.

Everyone on their feet scattered, including the officer with the babe in arms. The groggy guard began to stand up, but Ethan motioned him to remain where he was.

"You look like you're ready to keel over."

The man jutted out his jaw and came fully upright. "I messed up. I'm helping fix this."

If it can be fixed. But Ethan didn't utter the dark thought. "Understandable, but take it easy. We don't have time to be picking you up off the floor."

The officer nodded and tottered off to assist with the search.

Ethan headed for the room Lara and Maisy had shared. He stepped over the threshold, flicked on the light and scanned the area slowly. Maisy's diaper bag and Lara's go bag remained in the room. If Lara intended to run off and disappear, wouldn't she have wanted her belongings? He rifled through the bag and discovered the power-of-attorney and last-will-and-testament papers missing. Why take those and not the baby?

Then he checked Lara's cot and the playpen

Maisy had been sleeping in. The baby harness Lara had used in the forest was gone. It had been hanging from the corner of a chair next to the playpen. She took the baby harness without the baby? The clues got stranger and stranger.

His teeth ground together. *Lara, what is going on? Where are you?*

"She took it." Terry's voice came from behind Ethan.

He turned to find his partner standing in the doorway. "Took what?"

"The baby doll. It was sitting in the break room, but now it's gone."

Ethan's pulse jumped. "If Lara took the doll instead of Maisy, she *must* be going to a meeting set up by the Draytons. But that doll won't fool them for long. Once they discover the ruse, Lara's life won't be worth a thing."

Terry's frown said he agreed with Ethan's assessment. "If it helps, she left this in the doll's place." He held up a small brown-tinted glass vial in his gloved hand. "Must be the container for whatever she put in that officer's coffee. We'll have it tested and the container fingerprinted."

"But where did she get the drug?"

"Good question. I suspect the answer is

wrapped up in that fire alarm kerfuffle this afternoon."

"Beyond a doubt. To get Lara to take drastic action like this, the Draytons had to have blackmailed her somehow. We need to check on the status of Lara's mother. Since Maisy is safe here, that's the only leverage they might have on her."

Terry pulled his phone from his chest pocket and began to turn away.

"Is a technician on his way in to check the camera footage?" Ethan called after him.

"On the double." Terry turned back toward Ethan with a nod. "You'll never guess who's insisting on helping in this emergency."

"Alex Bingham, the kidnap victim?"

"Spot on."

"I thought he was on medical leave."

"He's cutting it short. Rabid for the opportunity to do something, anything, to get the Draytons."

Ethan grunted. "Can't say I blame him, and I've been told he's our best, which is what we need."

Terry walked away, already on his phone trying to find out the status of Lara's mother.

Ethan planted his hands on his hips and gazed around once more for anything he might have missed. *Come on, Lara, you had to have left us a few bread crumbs to guide us.*

Might she have left a note? Where would it be?

He hurried to the office he'd worked in this afternoon. At first glance, everything looked the same as he'd left it, but on second look—Ethan strode forward and snatched up the sticky note adhering to the corner of the desk.

He stared at the brief message. *Mother threatened. On my way to meet the Draytons. Follow me.*

"Clever girl," he murmured.

She left the drug vial to highlight the missing doll, and she left the note in place of the tracker they'd found inside the rattle. The serial number of the device was already in the marshal's system, courtesy of their failed attempt to find the buyer. A skilled tech should be able to use the serial number of the unit to locate the tracker wherever it was right now.

"Terry! I found something!" Ethan bellowed, and the man scrambled into the room almost before he'd finished speaking.

He held the note out toward his partner, who glanced at it and then at him with raised eyebrows.

"Follow her how?"

Ethan spread his lips in a shark grin. "Bingham better get here pronto and prove his reputation."

FIFTEEN

White-knuckled grip around the steering wheel, Lara drove through the night toward her meeting with Ronald and Vincent Drayton. During that horrible phone call while she was yet in the marshal's custody, the senior Drayton had directed her to a location a few blocks away from the courthouse. This vehicle had been waiting for her and the baby with an infant seat installed in the back. She'd also been told to bring with her all documents designating her as a caregiver or custodian to Maisy. That directive had come with his pledge to let her walk away once they had the baby and the documents.

As if Lara was about to believe such empty assurances! But she'd kept that thought to herself.

Now that she'd acquired the car and left the city, she was driving fast to stay on the strict timeline the senior Drayton had given her to reach the destination that had been preprogrammed into the car's GPS. Withholding the destination until she was already out of the marshals service's offices had prevented her from leaving that information in a note for Ethan. He was smart, though, and he would catch on to what she needed him to do. She had to hang on to that belief, or she'd lose her mind with fear.

Vincent had also warned her not to attempt to contact anyone from the phone they'd given her. It was being monitored by his people. Any reaching out for help via text or call would result in the death of her mother. She would also face the same consequence if she were even a minute late at the meeting site, ensuring she wouldn't dare stop anywhere on the way.

Vincent Drayton had dictated all the terms except one. Lara had stipulated that he and Ronald be present to personally take custody of Maisy. She'd absolutely refused to turn the child over to garden-variety thugs and stated she wouldn't make a move out of the courthouse without their pledge to be on-site. Vincent had seemed impressed by her caution and care for his granddaughter, which offered her a glimmer of hope that he and his son would meet the stipulation. If they didn't, this whole exercise would be a fruitless disaster, ending her and her mother's lives for nothing.

But no matter what, at least those evil people wouldn't get Maisy. She just needed to keep her adversaries from taking a closer look at the car seat. That doll would fool people only from a distance or in the dark. She'd have to think up any reason to put off letting them get near. Any delay or diversion would be golden, allowing Ethan and his rescue team an opportunity to catch up with her.

She reached out and touched the tracker she'd placed in the cup holder of the central console. *Ethan, you're on my trail, aren't you?*

On one level, the hours of travel crawled past, and she filled the hollow minutes with worship music from the radio and short, desperate prayers. On another level, the time flew by, and suddenly the GPS was telling her to make a turn onto a gravel road with her destination only a mile ahead. Minutes later, she arrived at a long driveway leading up to a building site.

Lara took her foot off the gas pedal and allowed the vehicle to coast up the driveway. Gravel crunched softly under the tires, and a pole light faintly illuminated the yard. Ahead and to her left was the burned-out shell of what must have been a house at one time. Ahead and to her right loomed a large barn, a bit rickety looking, but unscathed by the fire. A pair of large dark vehicles were parked in front of the structure. Golden light trickled from gaps in the barn door and shuttered windows. Her adversaries must be waiting for her inside.

Her pulse throbbed in her neck. She was about to come face-to-face with the people who had been trying to kill her and snatch Maisy. *God, be with me.*

She pulled the car over into a patch of shadows near the gutted house and sat still, struggling to draw in deep breaths. But she didn't dare delay for long, or the bad guys in that barn would come out after her. She couldn't have that.

With trembling fingers, she opened the car door and got out, custody papers in her hand. Balmy night air washed over her, carrying no trace of smoke, so the house fire must not have been recent. She locked the door of the vehicle, then looked down at the car keys in her hand.

Here goes.

With her best softball-star pitch, she flung the keys into the overgrowth around the house. If her adversaries wanted to get at the car seat and its occupant, they'd either need to find the keys or break into the car. The delay might come in handy. Of course, they might just shoot her down for hindering them, but it was a risk she'd have to take.

Squaring her shoulders, Lara trod toward the unwelcoming committee awaiting her in the barn. She hadn't gone a dozen feet when the barn door opened and a rifle barrel poked out, pointing in her direction.

"Where's my daughter?"

Lara's heart jumped at the harsh voice. From fear, yes, but also exhilaration. Ronald Drayton was present, and presumably, the man's father was also here. At least that much of her hasty plan had worked.

She kept walking slowly and waved the papers in the air. "Maisy is asleep." A truth she was reasonably confident about—she simply omitted *where* the infant was sleeping. "We conduct our business and you let me leave. Then you can collect the baby carrier out of the car."

"Stop right there," Ronald Drayton ordered, and Lara complied. "How do we know you've brought her if we can't see her?"

"Have patience, Ronnie," a more mature voice admonished from beyond the door. Vincent. "What purpose would it serve Ms. Werth to have failed to bring our sweet Maisy with her? But if it pleases you, I'll send Gary out to check that she's there."

A moment later, a large man with a big pistol stepped out the door. He scowled in Lara's direction as he passed her on the way to the car. Lara suppressed a shiver as she looked over her shoulder to follow the thug's progress.

Would the lifelike doll fool him? She'd placed a light blanket over the car seat, leaving only part of the doll's head and hair visible. The precaution would have to be sufficient. Her gut tightened as the hired gun leaned close to the rear window and bracketed his face in his hands to peer in.

The guy stood up with a grunt. "She's here," he called as he turned and headed back toward the barn.

"Good," said Vincent. "No need to disturb her yet. She will be fine there for the moment. Collect our guest and bring her inside."

The thug grabbed Lara's arm in a viselike

grip and dragged her toward the door. She suppressed her natural instinct to pull away. The better part of wisdom right now dictated she go along. She stumbled over the threshold into the well-lit interior of the cavernous building, and her throat clogged as if a fist had closed around it.

No fewer than six heavily armed thugs formed a half circle around a tall, dapper figure dressed in a suit. Next to him stood an equally tall but muscular younger figure wearing a button-down shirt and pair of slacks. Vincent and Ronald Drayton, beyond a doubt. Otherwise, the barn was empty. Odors associated with animals and machinery were mere whiffs of memory.

Vincent stepped forward and held out his hand. "The papers, please."

Without a word, Lara handed him the will and power-of-attorney documents. The man pulled out a lighter and lit a corner of the sheets. Wearing a faint smile that sent chills down Lara's spine, he gazed at the flames until they had nearly consumed the papers. Then he dropped the remnants and stomped on them with his expensive shiny shoes.

"May I go now?" Lara dredged up her

voice from beneath a layer of ice in her mind. *Ethan, where are you?*

"Certainly." Vincent's tone was cheery. "We'll all go."

He nodded toward the thug who still had her by the arm. The man grinned and pointed his gun at her. Lara went rigid. *This is it, God. See You soon.*

"Not in here!" barked Ronald. "For all the trouble she's caused us, I don't want her body or any trace of her ever found. Take her out back where there's a nice field to plant her. I'm going to get my daughter."

"Start the vehicles," Vincent told his men. "I'm going to greet my granddaughter. Keys, please." He held his hand out toward Lara.

She shrugged as casually as she could manage, which turned out more like a jerky-puppet movement. "I threw them in the grass."

The elder Drayton narrowed his eyes and then strolled past her. "No matter. We'll get the vehicle open in no time, with or without them."

Lara was dragged by the arm in the midst of the herd as they moved en masse toward the open barn door. But as they stepped outside, a pair of headlights suddenly blinked on, illuminating their faces. Everyone froze, and Lara's heart jumped. Ethan?

"Stop right there," a familiar female voice called out. "I'm a great shot, and at this range, I won't miss you, Ronnie, or you either, Vincent. Let Lara go."

"Izzy?" Her friend's name whispered from Lara's lips.

The thug who had her by the arm released her and lifted his gun. Lara began to edge backward to the rear of the group, but Ronald suddenly grabbed her and dragged her in front of his body as a shield.

"You shoot me, honey, you shoot your friend."

Lara struggled against the big man's hold, but his arm snaking over her shoulder and down to her waist was like a band of iron. In his other arm, he held his rifle in a one-handed firing position.

With an oath, Vincent darted behind one of his gunmen. A shot rang out, and the thug in front of Vincent abruptly hit the dirt. Then everyone with a firearm began blasting away.

Lara lifted her foot high and brought it down with all her might on Ronald's instep. The man yelped and loosened his grip. She jerked away from him and flung herself to the ground even as a feminine cry chilled her ears. Had Izzy taken a bullet?

"Stop firing," Vincent screamed at his men. "You could hit Maisy."

The dapper man began running toward the car Lara had driven to the site, but his son dropped to one knee and took careful aim with his rifle at his wife's vehicle. Still on the ground, Lara kicked out at the man's shin, and his shot went wild. Swearing, Ronald pointed his rifle down at Lara. Their gazes met, and the darkness in his core sent a shiver through Lara. His lips peeled back from white teeth, like a predator about to pounce, and the man's finger curled around his weapon's trigger.

A gunshot reverberated from a new direction, and Ronald screamed and flopped onto his back.

"Drop your weapons!" Ethan's voice cracked through the air. "This is the marshals service. You are surrounded."

Tears welled from Lara's eyes as her entire body melted into a puddle on the warm earth.

At the head of his fellow deputies, Ethan hurried forward, gun extended. His team had left their vehicles on the county road and crept up on the site as quietly as possible. When the shooting started without them, they rushed in. Isabelle Drayton showing up a step ahead of them had been a total stunner. Now she might be wounded or even dead. Men were converging on her vehicle. Terry and another deputy grabbed Vincent, who had reached the car Lara had driven and was yanking at the door handle.

"I want my granddaughter," he kept hollering over and over, even as the cuffs went on.

Ethan's gaze focused on the knot of thugs. As Drayton's crew dropped their weapons and raised their hands, Ronnie remained motionless on the ground. But where was Lara? There! Another figure was on the ground, but this one was moving.

Lara. Was she hurt?

His pulse hammered in his ears as he dropped down beside Lara, letting the others apprehend the hirelings. She was crying. He didn't blame her.

"Oh, Ethan!" She flung herself into his arms and buried her face in his chest.

He wrapped her close, murmuring comforting words. His body began to shake. Until this moment, he hadn't allowed himself to acknowledge how terrified he'd been since she'd gone missing. What did that say about how deeply he felt for this woman?

"Are you wounded?" he asked, stroking her hair.

"No." She pulled back slightly. "Just so relieved. All my emotions are gushing out." She lifted her head and gazed at him, eyes and cheeks moist. "You followed me. You found me."

"How could I do anything else?"

And he wasn't talking about doing his duty. Duty didn't cut it. Not now and not ever with Lara. But did she feel the same way? Now was not an honorable time to make a declaration of love or press her for one. Like she'd said, emotions were running so high.

Now that the Draytons had been apprehended, would the time for declarations ever come? After all, she was free to resume her life. Would she even want him in it as a reminder of all she'd been through?

If this was the only opportunity he had to express himself, he was going to do this one thing. As she gazed up at him with shimmering eyes, he lowered his mouth to hers. She went very still and then wrapped her arms around his neck.

Could his fellow deputies handle the arrests

without him? Yes, they could. Would they see him kissing the woman they'd just rescued? Yes, they would. Did he care? Not at all.

SIXTEEN

"How did you find me at that burned-out ranch?" Lara asked Izzy the question that had been knotting her brain for days now.

She stood by her friend's hospital bed, looking down at the woman's drawn face. Izzy's head was still wrapped in bandages from a bullet that had raked across her skull, but she'd been brought out of her weeklong induced coma yesterday. Lara had taken Maisy right away to see her mother and hadn't quizzed Izzy at all that day. But this morning, Lara's mother, who had flown in from Chicago, was looking after the baby so Lara could visit her friend and get some answers.

"That's an excellent question," said a familiar voice from the doorway.

"Ethan!" Lara pivoted to find the man moving toward her as panther-like as ever.

Her breathing hitched. She'd hardly seen

him since the night the Draytons were finally taken down—the night he'd kissed her as if his life depended on it. What had he meant by the kiss? Was he interested in a relationship with her now that the danger was over? Did she return the interest? Yes! Oh, yes!

Of course, Ethan's absence was understandable just maddening since questions lay unresolved between them. His occasional phone calls hadn't been optimal for getting answers about personal matters. He'd been shuttling between his office in Casper and state headquarters in Cheyenne—even flying to Chicago once—keeping his hand in the ongoing process of this major takedown of two of America's most-wanted fugitives. The arrest of Vincent and the death of Ronald were causing national and international reverberations. The entire Drayton network was being dismantled by multiple law enforcement agencies in the US and around the globe.

Ethan had told her that since Vincent's granddaughter was lost to him and his son was no longer among the living, the ruthless weapons dealer had morphed overnight into a broken man. He was no longer a threat to anyone, not even those who were slated to testify against him. Honestly? Lara would be delighted when the trial was over and the entire matter was in her rearview mirror. She was just getting used to feeling safe again.

Ethan came up beside her and offered a smile. Lara returned it, drinking in his presence for however long it might last.

"I was watching the courthouse." Izzy's words broke their eye contact, and Lara looked down at her friend.

"You were what?"

"That cop car and helicopter escort you received from the national forest to the US Marshals Service headquarters got media attention, so I knew where you were. And I knew Ronnie and Vinnie would find a way to get at you there. So I watched and I waited. Then when you left the courthouse with that Maisy-look-alike doll, I followed you."

"You knew I wasn't carrying Maisy?"

"Puh-lease." The word was a verbal eye roll. "I had binoculars on you and was close enough when you walked under a streetlight to see the hair on that supposed baby in the infant sling. Don't you think I know better than anybody my daughter's particular shade of red?"

Lara smiled. "Like nobody but a mother

would. And you still followed me, knowing Maisy was safe?"

Izzy scowled. "Yeah. *You* weren't safe, and I got you into this mess, so I needed to get you out."

"You're a brave woman," Ethan said.

"And a good friend," Lara added.

"Between your actions and Lara's stalling tricks," Ethan continued, "you two bought me and my team necessary seconds we needed to get in place."

Izzy wrinkled her nose. "I have no recollection of any gunfight. The last thing I remember was turning off onto the gravel road near the ranch."

Lara glanced up at Ethan. "The doctor says the memory loss isn't unusual with a head injury."

He nodded. "What I would like to know, Mrs. Drayton—"

"Izzy. And I'll be officially taking my maiden name back again as soon as possible. I had no idea who that man was when I married him. Please believe me."

Lara's heart throbbed. She could absolutely empathize with a woman fooled in a relationship.

"We do believe that, Izzy" Ethan said.

"You're not in any trouble, but we are going to need a comprehensive statement from you as soon as you're up to giving it. But what I'm curious about is why you decided to bring Maisy to Lara? I understand you hadn't seen each other in a decade."

"Good question." Lara echoed Ethan's earlier comment.

"Your mother." Izzy offered a small smile. "The day before Ronnie escaped from prison and came after Maisy, I ran into your mom at a beauty shop in Chicago. We recognized each other right away. She told me what a splash you're making in the art world—winning photography awards and everything. When Ronnie ambushed me in my apartment and I clobbered him with a lamp, I was frantic to think of a safe place to run with my baby. Then I thought of you and remembered where your mother said you lived."

Lara spurted a laugh. "So I have my mother to thank for this adventure?"

"I'm very sorry my actions caused you so much trouble. I thought I was being clever picking someone neither Ronnie nor his father would suspect." Izzy pecked at a bit of imaginary lint on her blanket.

"You had no way of knowing Ronnie had

placed a tracker in the baby's diaper bag in case you ran." Lara reached over and squeezed her friend's hand. "It was my privilege to help keep Maisy safe."

Izzy looked up at Lara. "And I appreciate it more than you can possibly know."

"I can see you're still very tired," Ethan said. "Why don't I borrow your friend here for a while, and an officer will be in later to take your full statement?"

"Sounds like a plan." Izzy's eyelids were already drifting closed.

Ethan's touch on her shoulder drew Lara's attention.

"Come walk with me outside," he said.

Lara's core tensed. Was this going to be goodbye? Could she bear another parting on top of the prospect of saying farewell to Maisy?

Sure, she could return to her contented solitary life, but things had changed in these couple of weeks. *She* had changed. The prospect of entering a serious relationship with someone again had ceased to terrify her quite so much, but was Ethan interested in her in the same way? A single kiss in the heat of a fraught moment was hardly enough proof to go on. But there was only one way to find out.

Pasting a smile on her face, Lara nodded. "I'll be back later," she told Izzy and walked out of the room with Ethan close behind her.

The hallway was busy and the elevator nearly full as they rode down to the first floor, so conversation was minimal. At last, they stepped outside into a manicured lawn-and-garden area. Few people were out and about here, and no one was nearby. A welcome cool breeze brushed Lara's face and took the edge off the summer heat. Ethan strolled next to her, an unusual tightness in his gait.

He glanced over his shoulder and then down at her. "I guess I forgot to ask Isabelle a question that particularly interests me."

"What's that?"

"Why she fled the hospital the first time when law enforcement was protecting her."

Is this why he'd asked her to take a walk with him? To question her about Izzy? Or was he stalling?

She sent him a sidelong look. Were those tension lines bracketing his mouth? Something was up. But what?

"I can answer that question," she said, "because I asked her the same thing before you arrived. Evidently, she was too afraid of Ronald and his father to stay where her location was known. Izzy was all too familiar with their resources, and she didn't trust your people to protect her. She bolted."

"I guess I can understand that." Ethan nodded. "As everything turned out, it was probably a good thing your friend was on the loose."

Silence fell once more, and something like a spring wound tighter and tighter in Lara's middle.

"Why are you here, Ethan?" she finally burst out.

A wry chuckle gusted from him. "I'm not very good at this, am I?"

"Thus far, I've never noticed anything you're not good at."

"Then you can count this as the first time, but hopefully not the last time… I mean, I hope we'll be around each other enough for you to notice more of my faults."

Lara stopped and turned in front of him, bringing them to a near collision. She stared up into his face as they stood bare inches from one another. "You *want* me to find fault with you?"

"No, that's not it." Ethan's face flushed.

"What I mean is, I want to spend time with you. Lots of it."

The coiled spring in Lara's middle began to unwind. "I've never seen you flustered." She let out a small laugh. "It's…refreshing and endearing. Are you talking about us dating?"

"If you're open to the idea. I know you've been burned in the past, but I'd like to have the opportunity to prove to you I'm not like—"

Lara pressed a finger to Ethan's mouth. "You've proved over and over that you're not like my ex-fiancé. Well, actually, you *do* have the same air of confidence and competence that drew me to him in the first place. But he was a fake and you're the real deal."

Lara's own words took her aback. Why hadn't she realized this sooner? Ethan was everything she'd thought she'd found in Matt. He was all of that and more. Exactly the man she'd been looking for all along. A rush of warmth filled her. It might take some time to get used to the novel idea of letting someone in, but she could trust Ethan Ridgeway with her heart.

Ethan's gaze warmed, and Lara's pulse beat faster.

He grinned down at her. "Then you won't hang up if I call you just to hear your voice?"

She grinned back. "I think I could squeeze a conversation with you into my busy schedule. But aren't you ever going to come around ringing my doorbell?"

"As soon as I wrap up this case, you're going to think I've taken up residence on your porch."

"You have to leave again?" Her smile faded. Of course, he had to go just when things were gaining momentum between them.

"Terry's waiting for me in the lobby." He took her elbow and guided her back toward the hospital door. "There is another bad guy out there we need to apprehend."

"Who?"

"We've discovered where Blaine Roberts is hiding out, and we're going to arrest him."

Lara blinked up at him. "The martial arts expert who knocked me out in the locker room?"

"The one and only."

"Be careful." She *couldn't* lose him now. "That man is lethal. I'm still amazed he didn't outright kill me when he could."

"If he'd been ordered to kill you, he would have done it quickly, efficiently and silently."

She shuddered. Ethan wrapped an arm around her shoulders, and she leaned into his warmth and sturdiness.

"But then," she said softly, "if he'd killed me, I wouldn't have been available to take Vincent Drayton's call. Getting me to deliver the baby was the point of it all."

"Exactly. Just like I've known from the start, you're smart as well as gorgeous." Ethan halted short of the door and took both of her hands in his. "This rush of activity will be over soon. Then I want to begin courting you in earnest."

"Courting?" She wrinkled her nose and quirked a teasing smile at him. "Such an old-fashioned word for a contemporary guy."

He chuckled. "Sometimes old-school is good. You're worthy of every honor and respect I can show you. Let me begin with this."

Ethan lifted one of her hands and brushed her knuckles with his lips. Lara's entire arm tingled at the feathery touch. If this was romantic Ethan, she could hardly wait for more of this courting business. She gaped at him with wide eyes and open mouth, words escaping her.

"Until later." He grinned. "There's no doubt about it. You are extra beautiful wearing a blush."

* * *

Three days later, Lara jerked awake in her Jackson home and sat up in bed. Maisy was crying. Lara glanced at the clock on her nightstand. Six, right on the nose. Smiling, she stuck her feet into a pair of mule slippers at the side of her bed. Then the crying abruptly stopped.

Lara crept to her door, opened it and leaned her head out. A murmuring voice from the other bedroom let her know that Izzy had felt up to rising and caring for her own child. A heaviness took up residence in the pit of Lara's stomach. Maisy's care was already transitioning from her to her friend, the child's mother. That the transition was right and good did nothing to ease Lara's sense of loss. At least the final separation had been postponed.

The doctor had advised against Izzy returning to her apartment in Chicago to care for her child alone. The woman had suffered a major head trauma and shouldn't be on her own yet, particularly not with an infant depending on her. Lara had stepped forward eagerly with an offer for her friend and Maisy to stay at her house until Izzy was fully recovered.

"Anything to get out of this hospital," Izzy had said with a wink in Lara's direction.

So Lara had brought Izzy to her house to stay until Izzy was fully recovered. It was just the three of them at Lara's home in Jackson. Her mother had headed back to Chicago, where planning a charity event desperately needed her attention. But Mom had promised to visit soon. Lara had no doubt her mother would arrange for the visit to happen while Maisy was still in residence. Should she feel slighted that an infant was the main attraction rather than her? Maybe, but she didn't. Lara totally got it. She and her mother were on the same page about precious Maisy.

Ethan had been MIA since that day he'd stopped briefly to visit at the hospital, and Lara missed him like a necessary appendage. Reliving that wonderful conversation about them dating occupied her mind while she showered and dressed for the day.

On her way to the kitchen to start breakfast, the doorbell rang, and Lara gasped and jumped a little. With measured steps, she headed for the door and put her eye to the peephole. Last time she'd opened without checking to see who was on her porch, she'd wound up with a gun in her face.

Ethan!

Lara pulled the door wide. The man stood there, tall and broad shouldered and so handsome her heart expanded enough to hurt her ribs. He wore civilian jeans and a casual polo shirt, so he must be off duty. Finally. Smiling, he held out a colorful bouquet of daisies, wildflowers and greens, exactly the kind of flowers she'd told him were her favorites during their time together in Bridger-Teton National Forest.

"You remembered! They're gorgeous." She accepted the bouquet and buried her nose in the fragrant blooms.

"I remember everything about those days at the cabin." The tenderness in his gaze drew Lara's heart like the warmth of the sun on a tender blade of grass. "Thinking about seeing you again has kept me working like a madman to wrap up my part of the case so I could be here instead of everywhere else."

Lara laughed. When was the last time her laughter had been so carefree? She couldn't honestly remember.

"Come on in." She stood aside. "You're just in time to join us for breakfast and then help me play with Maisy."

"I think I can handle that assignment."

He chuckled as he stepped over her threshold. "But first, if you don't mind." He moved closer and gently put his arm around her waist.

She gazed up into his eyes. "I don't mind."

"I need to warn you, I'm in love with you, Lara Werth."

"And I'm gladly, happily in love with *you*."

He lowered his lips to hers. Heart singing, Lara rose up on her tiptoes to meet his kiss. That old saying about fireworks exploding had nothing on this moment. It was true. There was no room for fear where love had come to stay.

EPILOGUE

Six Months Later

Newly elected Teton County sheriff Ethan Ridgeway signed off on the last report from his deputies and put the sheet in the outbox on the corner of his desk. Smiling, he sat back and gazed around his office. The room wasn't big or fancy, but it was up-to-date, efficiently organized and came with its own coffee machine—huge perk, no pun intended.

Late in the summer, when the former sheriff had announced he would be retiring at the end of his term, Ethan had thrown his hat in the ring. It had been a risky move for both his career with the US Marshals Service and for his relationship with Lara. He'd known if he won, he'd be changing career paths. He was fine with that, provided Lara said yes when he asked her to marry him later today. If she said no, it would be awkward with him as sheriff in the same town.

Yet, the joy in her eyes when he'd told her he was thinking about moving to Jackson and running for the office had made the decision for him. At that point, they'd been dating for only a couple of months, and popping the question had seemed premature. Thankfully, a former deputy US marshal had proved to be an attractive candidate for the citizens of Teton County. Now, four months later, here he was, sworn in as sheriff, and he wasn't waiting any longer for the moment of truth between him and Lara.

He opened his desk drawer, pulled out a square jeweler's box and tapped the top with a firm finger. "Don't say no."

Then he rose to head home and change for his date with Lara tonight. Funny how nervous he was. Their feelings for each other had done nothing but grow steadily over time, but he was under no illusions how difficult it had been for Lara to conquer deep-seated relationship fears. Those kinds of inner wounds took time and effort to heal thoroughly, and they persisted in little ways, cropping up out of the blue, despite people's best intentions. He understood that. Lately, her signs of caution had grown few and far between, but he still couldn't be sure he wasn't rushing things, at least in her mind. He'd even settle for a long engagement if she'd just wear his ring.

An hour later, his breath puffing out steam in the cold January air, Ethan rang Lara's doorbell. The door sprang open almost immediately, and a beaming Lara stood on the other side.

"You'll never guess what's happened," she cried.

"What is it?" Ethan's heart did a little jump.

She grabbed his hand and pulled him over the threshold. He shrugged out of his winter jacket and hung it on the coat tree in the foyer. Then she threw her arms around him, and he gladly returned the hug.

"It's absolutely wonderful." She gazed up at him with a brilliant smile.

"What is?"

Laughing, she released her hold around his waist and performed a little twirling dance into the living room area. The full skirt of the knee-length dress she was wearing swished around her.

She stopped and lifted her hands in the air. "Isabelle has had enough of Chicago with all its bad memories. She grew fond of Jackson when she stayed here, so she and Maisy are moving."

"To Jackson?"

"Yes! That's what I said."

"That's what you implied." Ethan grinned. "Just making sure I have my facts straight."

Lara stepped up to him and placed her palms against his chest. "Ever the lawman."

Taking advantage of the moment, Ethan pulled her close. "So we'll have the pleasure of the amazing Maisy's company indefinitely."

"Awesome, isn't it?"

"Better than awesome. But I have some news of my own."

"What news?" Her expression sobered.

"Well—" his gaze fell away from hers "—it's more like a question I need to ask you." Why did that box in his pocket suddenly weigh a ton?

"You know you can ask me anything."

He couldn't get a better invitation than that. Releasing her, he stepped back. He felt like a gangly, awkward teenager, but he managed to kneel in front of her anyway.

Her jaw dropped and both hands flew up to cover her open mouth. Was that a sheen of tears suddenly washing over her eyes? Should he take that as a good sign?

Ethan finally muscled the box out of his pocket. He mentally kicked himself. Should have taken it out before he knelt. But at last, he extended the box up toward her and popped open the lid.

"Lara Werth, will you marry me?"

A sob left Lara's lips.

"Don't worry. I'm not pressuring you to set a date," Ethan babbled on. "However long you want the engagement to be, I'm fine with that. I only hope you can—"

Her forefinger across his lips effectively stopped more words as she dropped to her knees next to him. "You wonderful man, of course I'll marry you. The sooner the better. And I don't want a big wedding. Just get my mom out here…and Isabelle and Maisy. And Jake too, since he helped us so much."

"And Terry," Ethan put in, grinning fit to burst. "And Rogan and his wife, Trina. Rogan would shoot me if I left him out of my wedding when I was best man for his."

"Invite anyone you want but do it fast. I can hardly wait to start our life together."

He took the ring out of the box and slid the circlet onto her finger. It fit perfectly. Lara gazed down at the symbol of their fresh commitment, her eyes sparkling like the diamond he'd given her.

Ethan lifted her chin and lowered his head. Their first kiss as an engaged couple. A pledge of many more to come.

* * * * *

If you enjoyed this book, look for these other stories by Jill Elizabeth Nelson:

Lone Survivor
The Baby's Defender

Dear Reader,

What a high-speed romance for Lara and Ethan as they raced through a harrowing situation. I'm so glad you came along for the ride. I hope you enjoyed getting to know them as they worked through their past traumas even as they experienced new dangers and challenges.

As with all my books, it is my prayer that this story strengthens people's faith and blesses their hearts, even as it entertains them. In this adventure, I hope you discovered—or rediscovered, as the case may be—the power of love to overcome fear. Like Lara muses toward the end of the story, 1 John 4:18 says, "There is no fear in love; but perfect love casteth out fear."

Again, thank you for joining Lara and Ethan on their hair-raising, but faith-developing and romantic, journey. I hope you will decide to accompany my other characters on their journeys in my past or future novels. Information about those can be found on my website: www.jillelizabethnelson.com. Also, I invite you to connect with me on my Facebook page:

www.Facebook.com/jillelizabethnelson. author. God's amazing blessings be with you, dear readers.

Until next time...
Jill

Get 4 FREE REWARDS!

We'll send you 2 FREE Books plus 2 FREE Mystery Gifts.

Love Inspired books feature uplifting stories where faith helps guide you through life's challenges and discover the promise of a new beginning.

FREE
Value Over
$20

Get 4 FREE REWARDS!

We'll send you 2 FREE Books plus 2 FREE Mystery Gifts.

Harlequin Heartwarming Larger-Print books will connect you to uplifting stories where the bonds of friendship, family and community unite.

FREE Value Over **$20**

Visit
ReaderService.com
Today!

As a valued member of the Harlequin Reader Service, you'll find these benefits and more at ReaderService.com:

- Try 2 free books from any series
- Access risk-free special offers
- View your account history & manage payments
- Browse the latest Bonus Bucks catalog

Don't miss out!

If you want to stay up-to-date on the latest at the Harlequin Reader Service and enjoy more content, make sure you've signed up for our monthly News & Notes email newsletter. Sign up online at ReaderService.com or by calling Customer Service at 1-800-873-8635.

RS20